THE WEDDING AT SEAGROVE

RACHEL HANNA

To my wonderful readers who send me the sweetest messages and love my characters as much as I do. I'm eternally grateful for your support!

CHAPTER ONE

Julie stared out over the rolling waves, Vivi firmly attached to her hip. She loved when Meg and Christian would allow her to keep her granddaughter. Lately, since Christian was working more hours and Meg had decided to go back to school at the local community college, Julie had gotten plenty of time to spoil her new grandbaby rotten.

The sun was starting to set in the sky beside the inn, and she knew Dawson would be calling her in to eat dinner any time now. Lucy was cooking up fried chicken and homemade biscuits tonight, complete with her peppery sawmill gravy, and Julie definitely didn't want to be late for that.

Vivi was growing so fast and almost crawling now. Her first Christmas had been so fun, watching her eyes light up when she saw the twinkling lights of the Christmas tree at Julie's cottage. Of course, her first picture with Santa Claus hadn't been so great. The photographer captured her terror as her face turned all shades of red and tears streamed from her eyes. Julie had tried to convince Meg that it would be a funny family memory one day, but Meg was disappointed nonetheless. She'd wanted a cute photo of Vivi looking at Santa for her Christmas card, but that didn't work out at all.

Now that winter was almost gone, Julie was looking forward to the warmer temperatures of springtime so she could build sandcastles with Vivi. It had been one of her fondest memories as a kid when they would take a yearly trip to the beach and she and Janine would have a competition of who could build the best sandcastle. Julie had always won, and it usually ended with Janine kicking over the winning display and stomping off in a fit. Ah, memories.

Vivi bucked and kicked on her side, wanting to go closer to the water. She was used to it already as they all spent so much time there. Even in winter, which wasn't too harsh in the lowcountry anyway, they spent most weekends having picnics or cookouts at the inn. Vivi loved it when Christian would hang her over the lapping waves and dip her toes into it.

"Not now, little one," Julie said, lightly tweaking her nose. It was hard to believe she was already eight months old. In the last week, she'd started a version of crawling that looked something like a crab that was missing a leg. As the days went on, she was getting better and better, and soon she'd be hard to stop.

Meg was going to school three days a week, and Julie sometimes had to take Vivi with her to the bookstore. For such a small island, she sure was able to keep herself busy between running the bookstore, helping Dawson with the inn and keeping her new granddaughter. But she'd never been happier in her life than she was right now.

Julie turned to look back at the inn. Dawson had done such a great job with the place since opening it a few months ago. The guests loved him, as did everyone he met, it seemed. Lucy was having a ball trying out new recipes and tweaking old ones, and Julie loved being her taste tester every now and again.

The worst part of the last few months was how much she'd missed Dixie. Right after Thanksgiving, Dixie and Harry had set off on their adventure of traveling around the country together. Occasionally, Julie got a postcard from some tourist destination, but Dixie mostly kept in touch with texts and video chats. It still wasn't the same as having her there live and in person. Julie missed their talks and Dixie's no-nonsense advice.

But, she had her mother there now. SuAnn had done surprisingly well in her efforts to keep her nose out of everyone's business. Sure, she said things. She would *always* say things. Julie and Janine had learned to cut her some slack, and she'd learned that her girls had boundaries. It was a work in progress.

Julie leaned down and held Vivi's hands, allowing her to kick her little feet on the surface of the sand. She didn't think Vivi would be crawling long before she learned to walk. After all, Meg had started walking at only ten months, and Julie definitely hadn't been ready for that.

"Well, there are my two best girls," Dawson said as he walked up behind them. He kissed Vivi on the head before sneaking a peck on Julie's lips. Sometimes, she just loved those sweet little moments with Dawson. Michael had never been the type to cuddle or snuggle, but Dawson was all about those things.

"Hey. I thought you were helping Lucy with dinner?"

He laughed. "She kicked me out of the kitchen."

"Kicked you out? What was the infraction?"

Dawson reached over and picked up Vivi, swinging her

into the air and then blowing raspberries on her cheek. "Apparently, my momma never taught me any manners because I stuck my finger in her apple butter to taste it."

"Oh, Dawson... You know better!"

"That's what she said." He chuckled as he handed Vivi back to Julie. She loved seeing him interact with her granddaughter. He treated her like she was his own, and sometimes that made Julie a little sad. Knowing that Dawson may never be a father tugged at her heartstrings. He never said anything about it, but she knew he felt a void in his heart after losing his only child so many years ago.

"Meg should be picking Vivi up in an hour or so, and then we can have the evening together," Julie said, smiling up at him.

"Sounds perfect. How about a movie under the blankets on the porch?" Since installing an outdoor theatre area, they often spent evenings watching their favorite films together. Julie had forced him to watch "Gone With The Wind", and he'd made her watch every John Wayne movie known to man. But she didn't mind. Spending her evenings cuddled up to a handsome Southern man by a fire pit wasn't a bad way to spend her time.

"As long as you feed me first, of course," Julie joked. She'd already gone up a pant size from eating Lucy's food, so she needed to start adding more salad to her diet before she had to buy a whole new wardrobe. Dawson hadn't seemed to notice.

"Of course," he said, taking Vivi from her arms again and hoisting her up into the air. Vivi giggled the whole time. "Let's head to the house. Lucy might question your manners too if we're late."

~

William stared at the computer screen, his new reading glasses on the tip of his nose. Sometimes, he felt like he was aging way too fast. The gray hairs coming in around his sideburns wasn't a welcome thing to see, although Janine had told him salt and pepper hair made him look sexy and distinguished. He wasn't sure he believed her.

"You look deep in thought," Janine said as she walked up behind him. He often worked in her office at the yoga studio since he didn't have an office of his own anymore. She didn't really need it anyway. He did most of her bookkeeping for her, and she much preferred being on the hardwood floor teaching her students to bend in the oddest directions.

He took off his glasses and rubbed the bridge of his nose. The stupid new glasses might have been necessary, but they were leaving a permanent red imprint. He'd have to take them back for the second time to get them adjusted.

"Oh, just trying to make sense of these numbers. I have a client who wants to spend way less to market her new skincare line, but wants to make twice what she did last year. Those numbers don't add up."

Janine smiled sadly. "You work so hard. Why don't you do a meditation with me? I promise it'll make you feel better."

William pulled her arm until she was seated on his lap. "I know what will make me feel better," he said, pressing his lips to hers. Janine giggled and stood up.

"Oh, no you don't! I have a class in a few minutes, and they aren't going to catch me in here making out with my bookkeeper!"

William's eyes widened. "Oh, is that what I am to you? A bookkeeper?" he said, standing up and poking her in the side. Janine cackled. He'd never met anyone as ticklish as she was, and he liked to take advantage of that as often as possible.

Janine laughed as she trotted back toward the front door of the studio. She was like a little butterfly, always flitting about here and there. Nobody in his life had ever had more energy than that woman. Of course, she attributed it to her yoga and meditation, as well as her healthy eating. But, he thought maybe God just made her that way, so full of life and enthusiasm.

He sure could use some of that enthusiasm right now. The few clients that he'd signed to his new marketing firm were unreasonable. One didn't want to pay for his work, so William had to hire a collection agency. Another one wanted him to create an entire marketing campaign for pennies, it seemed.

As much as he loved using his marketing skills, sometimes he wished he'd been talented in some other area too. Janine was living her dream, and he was just getting by. Maybe some people just didn't get to live their dreams. He loved her with all of his heart and soul, and she was a big part of his dreams, but he wanted more for his career. He wanted to smile and look forward to going to work in the mornings.

"Look what Momma just brought by," Janine said, standing back in the doorway again. She was holding something wrapped in aluminum foil on a plate. "Her peach pound cake! Can you believe it? I've been waiting all week for this!"

She was itty bitty, but Janine could put away the desserts. They were her guilty pleasure, especially since

SuAnn had opened the bakery next door. All he smelled all day long was the thick scent of sugar hanging in the air. How anyone concentrated on doing yoga was beyond him.

"We can have that for dessert tonight," he said, smiling.

Janine waved her hand at him. "This girl isn't waiting until dinner. I'm going to cut a quick piece before class. You want any?"

"No, but thanks. Try not to eat the whole thing before tonight, okay?" he said, winking at her.

Janine put the cake down on the desk and slid back onto his lap, her short legs dangling off one side. "Honey, you know your business will be successful, right?"

"I'm starting to wonder."

She kissed his nose. "I have faith in you, and I always will."

"I know, and you'll never know how much I appreciate that."

She hugged his neck and then slid off his lap again, taking the poundcake with her. "You sure?" she asked, holding it up again.

"I'm sure."

As he watched her walk away and disappear into the tiny break room area, he wondered what he'd done that had made him worthy of her. She was the most amazing woman he'd ever met, but he had a secret fear that one day she'd wake up and realize she was way too good for the likes of him.

~

SuAnn stood behind the counter and wiped at her brow. Even though it was early spring, it was already getting humid. She was trying her darnedest not to turn on the AC just yet, trying to save on her bills as a new business, but she figured she might cave in and turn it on if it got any hotter. The last thing she wanted was for the icing to start sliding off her freshly baked poundcake.

Today's special was her peach poundcake, and she'd already taken one to her daughter, Janine. There was just nothing better than fresh poundcake as far as she was concerned.

Being in Seagrove had been wonderful so far. She loved seeing her daughters everyday, and she saw her granddaughters a few times a week too. Of course, everyone was busy with their partners, and SuAnn had to admit she missed having a warm body to snuggle up with at night. Being divorced in her seventies sure wasn't something she'd expected.

Watching Dixie find new love had given her some hope, but most of the men she'd met so far were either married or had one foot in the grave. Were there any men left who didn't have a list of chronic ailments and a medicine cabinet full of prescriptions? She was still vibrant and wished she could find somebody who could match her energy. Everyone had always said Janine got her peppy personality from SuAnn, and she took pride in that.

The doorbell chimed and SuAnn popped her head up from behind the counter, where she'd been crouched trying to find a new bag of sugar.

"Hey, Grandma," Colleen said, waving at SuAnn.

"Hello, dear. How's your day been going so far?"

Colleen smiled and nodded her head toward Tucker, who was standing outside talking on his cell phone. "Any day is a good one when I get to spend it with him."

"Ah, young love." SuAnn chuckled. "So what are you two up to today?"

"We've got a big new project going on, so we're heading over to the beach to eat some lunch and brainstorm. Aunt Janine let it slip that you might have a new peach poundcake with my name on it?"

SuAnn rolled her eyes and laughed. "That daughter of mine never could keep a secret. She's got the loosest lips of anyone I know!" She slid a wrapped poundcake across the counter. "But, I did have one saved just for you. And Meg. And Julie..."

"Sounds like you've been a busy little bee, Grandma!"

She shrugged her shoulders. "Well, what else does an old woman like me have to do?"

Colleen stuck out her bottom lip. "Don't say things like that. You're just going through a transition. But, look how brave you were to take off on an adventure all alone!"

SuAnn knew she was trying to be inspirational, but hearing a twenty-something tell her about new adventures wasn't helpful. After all, everything a twenty-something did was an adventure. And if they messed up, they had decades to try over and over again. She didn't have that kind of time.

Truth be told, she was jealous of Dixie and how she'd been able to strike out on a new adventure with a new love. She wished she was so lucky.

"Don't worry about me, sweetie. I'll be just fine." SuAnn forced a smile as she watched Colleen walk back out of the bakery. Tucker slid his arm around her waist, kissed her cheek and then waved at SuAnn through the window. Young love or not, she was feeling envious of everyone she knew these days.

As she bent back down to look for that bag of sugar

again, she heard the door chime. Wanting to let out a curse word, she zipped her lips and stood back up.

A woman she'd seen around town was standing there. She hadn't come into the bakery before, but SuAnn had noticed her a few times looking through the window. They were about the same age, although the woman dressed more like a matronly old church lady than SuAnn ever would.

"Can I help you?"

"Why, yes," the woman said with the thickest Southern accent SuAnn had ever heard. She made Dixie sound like she was from up north. "I'm Henrietta Bankston." The woman paused for a long moment, as if SuAnn was either supposed to know her or be impressed by her regal sounding name.

"Nice to meet you. I'm SuAnn."

The woman stared at her, as if she'd just made a major faux pas. "Yes, I'm aware. You must not be from around these parts?"

"I'm new in town, yes."

The woman nodded, a puckered smile on her face. The big hat she was wearing was covered in fake flowers with one big sunflower in the middle. She had on a floral, button-up silk blouse, an off white skirt and the ugliest sandals SuAnn had seen in ages.

"Dear, I'm the mayor's wife. My husband is Reginald Bankston. He also runs Seagrove Bank."

"I guess with a name like Bankston..."

"Yes, we've heard that joke many times," Henrietta said, cutting her off. This was not a woman who would appreciate SuAnn's sense of humor.

"Can I interest you in some poundcake? We have the best anywhere around."

Henrietta scrunched her nose. "No, thank you. I'm trying to watch my figure."

SuAnn couldn't help but look her up and down. She was about to pop out of her skirt, so she wasn't sure whose figure she was watching but it certainly wasn't her own.

"Then why are you here?"

Henrietta pulled a piece of paper out of her giant handbag and gave it to SuAnn. "Our annual Spring Fling is coming up. We're trying to get donations from local businesses for our silent auction. It's a good marketing opportunity."

SuAnn looked at the paper. "Oh, that sounds nice. I'd be glad to donate."

"We also have a pie contest, but it looks like you only make cakes?"

"Actually, no. I make all sorts of things."

Henrietta smiled slightly. "I don't want to brag, but I've won the pie contest every year for twelve consecutive years. I'd hate for you to feel bad if you don't win."

SuAnn chuckled. "Honey, I rarely lose anything I put my mind to."

The tension hanging in the air was palpable as the two women stared at each other for what felt like an eternity. Thankfully, the door chimed and a new customer came in.

"Well, I can see you're busy. You'll find all of the information there."

SuAnn folded the paper and stuck it in her apron pocket. "Have a good day, Hen," she said as she turned back toward the counter.

"Oh, it's Henrietta," she called back to SuAnn, correcting her.

SuAnn said nothing. Boy, this was going to be fun.

CHAPTER TWO

Meg stared at the book sitting in front of her on the kitchen table. While Christian rocked Vivi to sleep, she had a few precious minutes to study before heading off to bed herself.

It wasn't that long ago that she was at school in France, learning and soaking up culture at the same time. Now, she had a hard time making sense of the numbers on the page. Why had becoming a mother warped her ability to understand math?

"She's finally asleep," Christian whispered as he walked up behind her and kissed the top of her head. "How's the studying coming along, mon amour?"

Meg loved his thick French accent, especially when he used terms of endearment. "Well, I've come to realize that giving birth has made me an idiot."

"Do not say such things," he said putting his arms around her neck and kissing her cheek. "You are so intelligent, and you know this."

"Maybe I'm just not cut out for this. I mean, I have my poor mother taking care of my daughter, and what if I fail these classes? At the community college? I'm not even at a real university, Christian."

He sat down next to her and took her hand. "You think too much, my love. I know you can do this. Let me help you, okay?"

Meg smiled slightly. "But you don't teach math, sweetie."

He chuckled. "I remember enough. Now, show me what you don't understand."

~

"Your total is twenty-two forty-nine," Julie said as she rang up three books for one of her favorite local customers. Miss Bessie, as everyone affectionately called her, was ninety-two years young. She always came in with her long-time caregiver, Amelia, and she only came on senior discount day.

"And I did get my discount, didn't I?" she asked, as she always did.

"Yes, ma'am. You sure did," Julie said, as she always did.

This week, Miss Bessie was buying a cookbook, even though she didn't cook. She was also buying a bird-watching book, even though she could barely see. Julie assumed that Amelia read the books to her. This time, she was also buying a local history book.

"Miss Bessie, I noticed you picked out a history book this week. About Harriet Tubman?"

Bessie smiled as she leaned back in her wheelchair. "Oh, yes. You know, I was told as a small child that we share a bloodline with Harriet Tubman. Always made me so proud. I swear I stood two inches taller every time Momma said it."

"That is something to be proud of," Julie said, putting her books into a brown paper bag. Dixie refused to get plastic bags after seeing how detrimental they were to the local environment.

"You know, they used a local river to transport slaves to freedom."

"Really? I didn't know that."

"Oh yes. The Combahee River. I can just imagine my ancestors smelling the warm scent of the sweetgrass as they hid, hoping for freedom." She closed her eyes and smiled, her thoughts a million miles away.

"I can't imagine what that must've been like."

"Miss Bessie, we'd better get going. You don't want to miss bingo, do you?" Amelia said, putting her hands on Bessie's shoulders.

"Oh, Lord no!" Bessie said, cackling with laughter. She leaned in and looked at Julie. "I win almost every time."

Julie chuckled. "I bet you do. Have a good afternoon, Miss Bessie. See you next week!"

She watched Amelia roll Miss Bessie down the sidewalk and out of sight. Julie was so thankful for this town and its people. Every day, she got to talk to the most amazing individuals that she never would've crossed paths with back in Atlanta.

Sometimes, she thought about how different her life was now. It wasn't that long ago that she was married to a cheater, living in a big lonely house, interacting with the horrid women at her tennis club and thinking that was a great life. Now, she was living on a tiny low country island, seeing her daughters and granddaughter daily and head over heels in love with the man of her dreams.

"Anybody need a break?"

She turned around to Dixie poking her head out of the

back room. "What on Earth?" Julie said, running out from behind the counter and hugging Dixie tightly. She hadn't seen her in months, and it felt good to wrap her into a big hug.

"Thought I'd sneak in the back way so my fans wouldn't see me out front," Dixie joked. Gosh, she'd missed her sense of humor. When Dixie was around, she felt safe.

Julie pulled back and looked at her. She looked good and healthy. Mostly, she looked happy. "When did you get home?"

Dixie smiled. "About an hour ago. Harry told me to take a nice nap, but I wasn't about to go without seeing my girl!"

"Why didn't you tell me you were coming home today? I would've had a special dinner or something."

"That's exactly why! You're a busy lady... and grandma... these days. No sense in fussing over me."

Julie hugged her again. "I've missed you so much."

"Me too, sweetheart. It's good to be home again."

Julie finally let her go and they both sat down at the bistro table. "Tell me you're staying put for awhile?"

Dixie bit her lips. "For a bit. But, we do plan to take some trips this summer. Maybe not quite as long as this one."

"So, tell me everything! Where'd you go? What did you do?"

Dixie held up her hands. "Whoa, slow down there!"

"I'm sorry. I know you're exhausted from your trip. I just hope you had a great time."

"Oh, we did, hon. The best time of my life, in fact."

Julie grinned. "That makes my heart smile to hear you say that. I love you."

"And I love you too, darlin'." Dixie stood up and stretched her arms over her head. "I think I'll head home and take a nap. Plus, I need to take my Parkinson's medication. You know it has to be taken at the same times every day. Three times a day for me. What a pain!"

"I know. Take care of yourself. When you're ready to chat and tell me all the gossip from your trip, you know where to find me."

Dixie reached out and squeezed her hand. "And boy, do I have plenty of gossip to tell you!"

"I'm looking forward to it!" Julie said as she watched Dixie walk out the back of the store again. She held her hand to her chest and quietly thanked God for the amazing life she had.

~

"I still don't understand what you're looking for, Mom," Janine said as she watched SuAnn dig through yet another box.

"I know your sister must have it in here somewhere," she said, still staring into the old box of photo albums and family genealogy paperwork. How Julie had managed to get these boxes all the way to Seagrove and up into her attic, Janine would never understand. Of course, she was not one to hold onto things, having traveled the world so much. She'd been just as happy with her tapestry backpack and her favorite stainless steel water bottle.

"Why are you so frantic about it?"

SuAnn looked up at her. "Dear, I own a bakery. Why wouldn't I want to find our old family recipes?"

Janine shrugged her shoulders. "Maybe Julie has them in the kitchen?"

"I already looked there. Can you text her? I don't know how to do that on my phone."

"Fine," Janine said, rolling her eyes. No matter how many times they'd taught SuAnn how to text, she refused to even try. Janine typed out a quick text to Julie and then stood up to stretch. It was one of the hazards of being a yoga teacher, she supposed.

"Hand me that other box you brought down from the attic," SuAnn said, her hand reaching out. She hadn't seen her mother look this flustered in years. Why was she so frantic about looking for recipes?

"Mom, is the bakery not doing well or something?"

SuAnn looked up, a piece of her hair hanging between her eyes. She poked her bottom lip out and blew the hair upward. "It's doing great. Why would you ask me that?"

"Because you're acting like a chicken with its head cut off. Why the rush over finding these recipes?"

"Well, dear, they're priceless family heirlooms," she insisted, looking back down.

"Hogwash! You're up to something, Mother. I can always tell."

SuAnn shook her head. "You're crazy, Janine. I'm simply trying to preserve our family heritage."

"God's gonna strike you down in a minute," Janine said, rolling her eyes. She handed SuAnn the other box. If there was one thing she knew about her mother, it was that she got nervous and agitated when she was up to no good. The last thing Janine wanted was for her mother to be causing trouble in their new hometown.

SuAnn started digging through the new box, her hair falling back into her face again. "Honestly, Julie needs to get an HVAC guy out here. This living room is as hot as blue blazes!"

Janine walked over and checked the thermostat. "Mom, it's seventy-two degrees in here. That's hardly hot."

SuAnn swiped her hair out of her eyes again. "Well, it sure feels hotter."

"That's because you're acting like a lunatic digging through these boxes," Janine said, sitting down next to her. "Mom, listen to me."

SuAnn sighed and looked at her. "What?"

"I know something's going on. Why don't you just tell me what it is and..."

"I found them!" SuAnn said, her eyes cutting over to the box while Janine was talking. She grabbed a stack of worn, slightly brown papers that were held together by a rusty paperclip and held them to her chest. "I thought they might be lost forever."

"Mom."

"What?"

"What is going on? And don't say nothing."

SuAnn blew out a breath. "Okay, fine. I'm trying to be a better person, so I'll tell you the God's honest truth."

"I'd prefer that."

"This horrible woman came into my bakery. Terrible fashion sense, a snooty attitude, perfume that would peel the paint off the walls..."

Janine rolled her hand in the air. "Get to the point faster."

"Anyway, turns out she's the mayor's wife. Her butt was so stuffed in that God-awful skirt of hers that it looked like two beach balls were trying to escape. I wanted to get a safety pin and try to pop them."

"Mom! What does this story have to do with those recipes?" Janine was growing frustrated, even if her mother's description of the mayor's wife was entertaining.

SuAnn smiled sheepishly. "There's this pie baking contest."

"Oh no."

"Look, I don't have much else going on in my life right now. Let me have this."

"Mom, you're terrible when it comes to competitions. Don't you remember how insane you'd get every time I had to sell Girl Scout cookies? They were giving away an umbrella, and you just about mowed down poor Mrs. Daugherty to get that space in front of the ice cream shop!"

"You won that umbrella, didn't you?" SuAnn said proudly.

"And remember when Julie took those modeling classes, and when she walked the runway you yelled so loud that they threw you out of the auditorium? Poor Julie was mortified."

"I wanted her to know I was there."

Janine laughed. "Oh, she knew you were there alright. But, my favorite was when we had the three legged race during field day when I was in fourth grade."

"I don't remember that."

"You hated Callie Rowland's mom."

"Oh, yes. That old cow, Delilah. She was the town tramp, sleeping with everybody's ugly husbands."

"You're telling me you don't remember purposely tripping her so we could win?"

SuAnn tried to hide the smile spreading across her face. "She landed like a big sack of potatoes right in that mud puddle."

Janine lightly smacked her arm. "You're terrible."

"I can admit now that it wasn't a nice thing to do, but I do still have fond memories of seeing the look on her face as she sat there in her fancy white capri pants and all that fake costume jewelry."

"Mom, you know you can't create chaos here, right? This is our new home, and we don't want drama."

SuAnn nodded. "I know. I'm not going to do anything like that, Janine. I'm really trying to be a better person. More accepting."

Janine rubbed her upper arm. "I know, Mom. But, is it really the best idea for you to get involved in a competition of any kind? It doesn't bring out your best side sometimes."

SuAnn stood up and slid the papers into her oversized tote bag. "I promise I'll behave, dear. I wouldn't do anything to ruin this new life I'm trying to build. I just wanted to have my grandma's pie recipes because nobody can possibly beat me if I use one of those."

Janine walked her mother to the front door. "Remember, you want to make new friends here."

"I've never been very good at that, Janine. Plus, I have my two girls here. Why do I need friends?"

It made Janine sad to hear her mother say something like that. "Because you deserve it."

As she watched her walk to her car, she wondered what was going to happen when her mother entered that competition. She feared it wouldn't be good.

~

Colleen stared at the large bowl of candy in the middle of the conference room table. She loved chocolate. It didn't matter what kind it was or what it was covered with. Chocolate covered strawberries, raisins, nuts - she'd eat any of them. These were just plain chocolates, but she still struggled not to grab a handful of them and shove them into her mouth. Thankfully, she was sitting next to Tucker, and he was holding her hand.

"Sorry to keep you both waiting," the woman said as she came into the room, shook both of their hands and sat down.

"No problem. I know you must be busy," Tucker said.

"Always. I wish I wasn't," she said, smiling sadly. "Our foster care system is overwhelmed, and it only seems to get worse with each passing year. So many kids in terrible situations. I swear I stay up most nights trying to figure out a solution, ya know?"

"Well, that's why we're here, actually," Colleen said.

"Oh?"

"We work in the toy invention business," Tucker said. He slid one of his business cards across the table.

"That must be very interesting," the woman said. "But, I don't quite see the correlation between toys and foster care?"

Colleen decided to take over. "We were thinking... actually, hoping... to use our skills to help get some of these kids adopted and provide a really great learning opportunity for them too."

"How so?"

"We'd like to propose a toy invention camp where a group of kids can come and Tucker will teach them about inventions, starting their own companies one day, marketing and so forth. Obviously, this would be more suited for older kids, maybe elementary ages and up. At the end of camp, we'd have a huge party and invite the public. You could be there with some of your staff to help facilitate meetings and give more information on becoming a foster parent, or, better yet, an adoptive parent."

The woman, who Colleen knew was named Amy Winston from her name tag, leaned back in her chair and tilted her head. She thought for a long moment.

"You know, that's not a bad idea at all. It's actually quite innovative."

Tucker looked at Colleen and smiled. "Our very good friend, Dawson Lancaster, owns The Inn At Seagrove. He has already agreed to let us host it on his grounds. He also has a nice big shop in the back of his property where we can do hands-on demonstrations for the toy invention classes. I'm planning on demonstrating how to draw inventions, and I'll even show them how I built one of my best-selling toys."

"So, do you think you could get ten to fifteen kids to participate?" Colleen asked.

"Definitely. I have a lot of boys and girls who would be a great fit for something like this. But..."

"But?" Colleen said.

"I have to ask... What would the cost be?"

Colleen and Tucker looked at each other and laughed. "We hadn't considered charging anything, actually," Colleen said.

Amy's mouth dropped open. "Really?"

"We just wanted to give back to the community and touch some kids' lives. We never thought about getting paid," Tucker said.

Amy stood up and pressed her hands together in a praying position. "God must have sent you because I can't think of a nicer offer!"

Colleen and Tucker stood up and Amy ran around the

table to hug them. They definitely hadn't expected that kind of reaction.

"I guess we better start planning?" Tucker asked.

"Yes! Oh, I can't wait to tell our board members. They're going to be so excited. Let's talk over email and finalize the date and details," Amy said.

"Sounds good. I'll be in touch soon," Colleen said as they walked toward the door. It felt good to be appreciated for trying to help the kids in her community, and it would be a few hours before anything could wipe the smile off her face.

CHAPTER THREE

There was nothing Julie looked forward to more than Sunday dinners. It was the one time of the week where she got to catch up with everyone. Life had been plugging along at a hectic pace recently, so she was looking forward to finding out what was going on with everyone.

"Can you put the rolls on the table?" Julie said, handing the basket to Janine.

"Is Mom coming?"

"Yes. She was able to get her new employee to cover for her this afternoon. She really needs a day off. I think it's starting to stress her out being at the bakery all the time."

"Well, if she could keep an employee and not run all of them off..."

Julie held up her hand. "I know. But, it's Sunday, and on Sundays we're all happy, right?"

Janine laughed. "Sure, sis. Whatever you say."

As they finished setting the table, everybody started filtering into the house. First Dawson and William, both of whom planted kisses on their respective partners, and then SuAnn, Colleen, Tucker, Meg and Christian. Julie was excited to surprise everyone with another guest.

"Welcome, everyone. I'm always glad to see your smiling faces on Sundays," Julie said, standing up as if she was presiding over an important meeting. She held up her glass of sweet tea. "In honor of this beautiful Sunday afternoon, I'd like to let you in on a little surprise..."

As soon as she said it, Dixie popped out of the laundry room, a big grin on her face. Simultaneously, everybody descended upon her, giving hugs and kisses on her cheek.

"Y'all make an old girl feel really loved," Dixie said, once everyone backed up a bit. "Is this what my funeral will be like?"

"Only if you pop up and surprise all of us," Dawson said, with a wink.

"I'll give it my best shot," she responded, winking back at him.

"I'm so glad you're home, Momma," William said, putting his arm around her. She buried her face in his chest.

"Me too, darlin'. Me too."

"Where's Harry?" Colleen asked.

"Well, Harry is at home nursing a sprained ankle. He stepped off the patio and just rolled it the wrong way this morning. Doc says it's not broken, but he has to stay off of it for a few days. That man hates to be lazy, so I expect I'll see him up and about by the time I get home," she said with a laugh.

"Come sit down and tell us all about your adventures these past few months," Meg said, patting the chair next to her. Dixie sat down and smiled.

"Okay, but let's pile our plates high with food first. I haven't had a home cooked meal in ages!"

As they laughed and passed dishes of food around, Julie swore she could feel her heart literally warming up in her chest. For her whole life, she'd imagined a family like this. Well, maybe not exactly like this, but this was better.

She had everyone in the world that she loved sitting at one table. Dawson, her daughters, her sister, her mother. And Dixie, her extra mother, as she called her. She just never said it around SuAnn because that would've been a recipe for disaster.

When she let her mind go back to those years of marriage to Michael, it almost scared her to think of what her life would be like if he hadn't destroyed their family. At the time, she'd thought it was the worst thing that had ever happened to her, but now she wouldn't trade this new life for anything.

"So, where's the first place you and Harry went?" Janine asked as she took a bite of her salad, the loud crunch of cucumber echoing down the table.

"Well, we went to Gulf Shores, Alabama first. Nice area. Beautiful water and white sandy beaches. Then, we made our way over to New Orleans for a few days. What a hoot!"

"You didn't get on one of those balconies and flash somebody, did you?" William asked, looking at her speculatively.

"As much as I'd love some of those beaded necklaces, I didn't want to get arrested. Besides, if I took these old girls out of my bra, they'd splat right on the ground!" Dixie roared with laughter as William put his face in his hands.

Julie couldn't help but laugh too. Dixie had the best sense of humor of anyone she'd ever known. And the filter between her brain and mouth was missing completely.

"I feel your pain," SuAnn mumbled under her breath.

"Mom, don't you start too," Janine said with a chuckle. "We don't need y'all comparing bosom issues."

"Bosom?" Meg said, rolling her eyes and laughing. Vivi wiggled beside her in the highchair that Julie kept at her house.

"Anyway... Dixie, tell us more about your trip," Dawson interjected. Julie smiled at him appreciatively.

"We just had the best time, I tell ya. We went as far west as Vegas, in fact," she said, looking down at her plate before taking a big bite of her yeast roll.

"Oh yeah? Did you do any gambling?" Colleen asked.

"Just some slots when we first got there. We actually parked the RV and stayed in a fancy shmancy hotel one night. They had a beautiful buffet and this great waterfall thing out front."

"Sounds very nice, Dixie," SuAnn said.

"It was. And they had a lovely honeymoon suite with a heart shaped bed and jacuzzi tub. Really helped my sciatica."

"Honeymoon suite? Why would you stay there? Was that all they had left?" William asked, staring at her.

"No. We, um... we chose it."

"Sounds like they just needed a little romantic getaway, William," Janine said, poking him in the side and grinning. "Sounds fabulous to me."

Julie noticed that Dixie wasn't looking up, and she seemed nervous. "Are you okay, Dixie? Do you need your medicine?"

Dixie shook her head and looked up slightly. "No, it's not that."

"What's wrong, Mom?"

She sucked in a long breath and blew it out slowly, before reaching into her pocket for something. Julie watched as she slid a gold band on her finger and held it up. Everything seemed to be moving in slow motion as every person around the table realized at once that Dixie had gotten married.

"We got hitched," she said softly, a reserved look on her face.

"What?" William said. Nobody else spoke or congratulated her, worried that William wasn't going to react well.

"We got married, son," she said, finally looking at him. "Harry is now my husband."

The silence was deafening, nobody knowing what to say or do until William made the first move. After all, he probably never expected his mother to remarry, especially since she'd said she wouldn't ever get married again. Johnny had been her one true love.

William put his napkin on the table and stood up, walking over to the window and looking out for a brief moment before finally coming back to the table. He stood next to his mother. "And I missed it?"

"It was very spur of the moment, William. We didn't plan this, I promise." She stood up, holding onto the chair, her nerves very apparent.

Slowly, a big smile spread across William's face. "I'm so happy for you, Mom!"

Julie swore she could hear everybody let out a collective sigh of relief as excitement and congratulations permeated the room. William pulled Dixie into a warm embrace.

"You mean you're okay that I got married again?" she asked, incredulously, as she looked up at him.

"Of course! Mom, I've wanted you to have a second chance at love most of my adult life. This is amazing news! I wish Harry was here to share in the celebration."

"Me too, son, me too," she said, as her eyes filled with tears. "I wasn't sure if I'd even tell y'all today, but I'm sure glad I did!"

Everybody took turns hugging her until they finally all sat back down. Dixie proudly displayed her new wedding ring and regaled them with stories of her recent traveling adventures.

Julie didn't know why her news was so surprising. This was how her Sunday dinners always went. There was never a dull moment with her crew, and she wouldn't have had it any other way.

~

Janine reached her arms high into the air and then swept forward, her head hanging as her hands rested on the hardwood floor. She loved forward hangs. They allowed the tension that built up in her neck to release after a long day of teaching.

People often assumed that she, as a yoga teacher, would live a stress free lifestyle, but nothing could have been further from the truth. She loved having her studio, but managing the business sometimes wore her down. William helped, but she didn't want to rely on him, especially since he was so busy with his own new business lately.

She missed having frequent date nights, like they used to do before he started working so much. She would often find him sitting in the town square, working furiously on his laptop. But, he didn't seem happy. He seemed stressed, tense and worried much of the time, and that worried her.

"Long day?" she heard him say from behind as he walked into the studio.

"Every day is a long day, but you know I love it," she said, smiling as she pulled him into a hug. Burying her head in his chest at the end of her work day was one of her favorite things.

"I know you do."

They stood there for a moment before she pulled back and looked up at him. "What's up?"

"Nothing. Just tired. I made thirteen calls today. Got one potential client."

"That's great, right?"

He shrugged his shoulders. "I guess." He walked over and sat down on the rolling chair Janine kept in the corner of the teaching room. She sat on the floor, cross legged.

"William, you seem really unhappy with this new business. Maybe it's not the right thing for you?"

"What else am I qualified to do, Janine? I've been in this line of work since just after high school."

"You don't have to keep doing things that make you miserable, William. Look at your mom!"

"What do you mean?"

"She thought getting married again would mean her marriage to Johnny didn't matter, but she realized that she deserved a second act."

"But Mom is in her seventies, and I'm certainly not. I have to stick with what I know and try to build a lasting career. I can't just stop what I'm doing and pursue something else."

Janine leaned back a bit and crossed her arms. "And why not?"

"It's not mature."

"Do you think I'm not mature?"

He stared at her. "I think you're very mature. Are you trying to start an argument?"

She smiled slightly. "I'm saying that I do what I love, and I've made it a pretty good business too. What about your Mom?"

"What about her?"

"She loved reading and created a wonderful bookstore. And Dawson. He loved working on things and became a contractor. And Tucker loves toys so..."

"Yeah, I get it. But, I've always been more... straight laced."

She leaned up onto her knees and ruffled his hair until it was a mess.

"There."

"What did that accomplish?"

"I messed up that perfectly put together persona you've got going on, and you didn't die."

William chuckled. "What do you want me to do, Janine?"

"I want you to do what makes you happy. Okay, let's try a little exercise I learned in a personal development book one time."

"Oh, good Lord," he said, rolling his eyes.

"Humor me, okay?"

"Fine."

"Close your eyes." Unwilling to argue with her, William closed his eyes. "Now, try to clear your mind by taking a few deep breaths. In through your nose and out through your mouth." He did as she said. "We want to access your subconscious mind, and to do that I'm going to ask you some questions, and I want you to answer me with the first thing that comes to mind, okay? No filtering. Just be quick and honest."

"Okay."

She decided to ask him some easy questions first just to get him in the zone. "What's your favorite color."

"Blue."

"What's your favorite movie?"

"Die Hard."

She wanted to laugh at that last answer, but didn't want to mess up the exercise. "What's your favorite food?"

"Steak."

"If you could wake up and do any career tomorrow, what would it be?"

"Fishing guide."

Suddenly, William's eyes popped open. They stared at each other as a grin spread across Janine's face. "There ya go!"

"You want me to be a fishing guide?"

"No. *You* want you to be a fishing guide!"

William stood up and walked across the room. "Janine, I can't do that. First of all, I haven't fished the marshes since I was a kid. Secondly, I have bills to pay like my rent, my car..."

She stood in front of him and put her hands on his arms. "You get one life, William. One. Your soul wants to be a fishing guide, and I'm going to help you get there. You helped me, now it's my turn to help you. Okay?"

"This is insane. You know that, right?"

"The most insane things always lead to the most amazing things."

He shook his head. "I'm not sure you're right about that."

~

Meg walked across the small community college campus and sighed. Going back to school was harder than she'd thought it would be. Vivi was teething again, and she'd kept Meg up all night again. Her eyes felt like they were going to close up on her whether she liked it or not.

"Hey there!"

She turned to see her friend, Darcy, standing next to the fountain. She was holding her son, Hatcher, on her hip as he leaned over and tried to reach the water spouting up into the air.

"Long time, no see!" Meg said. It had been weeks since she'd seen her only friend, with school and being a mommy taking up most of her time.

"I haven't seen you around the bakery lately."

Meg sighed and sat down on the edge of the fountain. Darcy tossed a penny over her shoulder and sat down, Hatcher wiggling on her lap. "School is killing me. I've recently learned that I might be an idiot."

Darcy laughed. "Girl, you're not an idiot. It's hard going back to school with 'mom brain'. I can't imagine doing this right now. Be proud of yourself!"

"I'm barely passing math. Christian has been trying to help me, but last night we both fell asleep during my homework session and poor Vivi was sitting in her high chair looking at us like we were the worst parents ever."

"Isn't your mom keeping her for you?"

"Sometimes. But, I feel bad asking her to keep her when I'm not actually in class. She has her own life too. Vivi is my responsibility, and I love being her momma. I do. Sometimes, I just need a break!"

"Listen, I'm happy to keep sweet little Vivi anytime, okay?"

"You're busy, Darcy. But, thank you."

"I'm not so busy that I can't help my friend. Listen, you and Christian pick a date night and let me keep Vivi. You can return the favor when school is out. Sound good?"

Meg smiled gratefully. "Our date night might consist of putting on our PJs, eating frozen pizza and staring at the TV."

Darcy stood up and put Hatcher back on her hip. "You do what you need to do, girl. No judgment here!"

Meg laughed and stood up. She lightly pinched Hatcher's fat little leg. "You seem to have it all together."

Darcy rolled her eyes. "Yesterday, I burst into tears because I couldn't get Hatcher to stop throwing his nasty baby food at me. I had prunes in my hair and had to wash it all over again."

"Good to know I'm not alone," Meg said, chuckling. "This morning, Vivi threw up all over my new shirt. I had to change, and I got to class ten minutes late."

"Motherhood!" Darcy said, laughing. "Well, I'd better get going. I signed up for this mommy and baby class over at the community center. I'm now regretting my life decisions."

Meg smiled. "You'll do fine."

Darcy started walking away. "I don't make friends well, remember?"

"Well, you've got me as a friend!"

Meg watched as Darcy walked away, Hatcher bucking around on her hip. She was so thankful to have someone who totally understood her life right now.

CHAPTER FOUR

Dixie was a little bit nervous. It was a rare event that William asked to talk to her privately. As much as she loved her son, their past issues were worrying her today. All those years they didn't speak, and now he wanted to talk to her? Maybe he was just putting up a good front at Sunday Dinner, and he really didn't approve of her marriage to Harry. Maybe he was about to break ties with her for good. The thought made her shudder.

She pulled the apple pie out of the oven and set it on the counter. William had always loved her apple pie, so Dixie had decided to make it just in case she needed a little extra something to keep him from being mad at her. After all, what else could he want to talk about?

Just as she heard the coffee finish brewing, William knocked on her front door. Ever since Johnny had died all those years ago, she'd gotten into the habit of keeping her doors locked. Seagrove was the safest community she could imagine, but she didn't want to take any chances.

"Hey, hon," she said as she opened the door. William smiled.

"Hey, Mom." He leaned over and gave her a quick hug before walking inside. At least that was a good sign. "Is that apple pie I smell?"

Dixie smiled as she followed him into the kitchen. "Of course. When my son calls a meeting with me, I figure it's never a bad idea to have pie on hand. Can I cut you a slice?"

"Sure," he said, sitting down at the kitchen table. She could see him out of the corner of her eye, fidgeting with his hands. He was nervous, and now she was too.

"Coffee?"

"Of course."

"Black, right?"

"The manly kind of coffee," he said, laughing as he recounted his father, Johnny, always saying that.

Thankfully, Dixie had kept some of Johnny's old coffee mugs, mainly his favorites. They were stained and mostly ugly, but she always liked serving William his coffee from one of those mugs. Anything to keep her beloved Johnny's memory alive.

Sometimes, being newly married felt like a dream. She adored Harry, and she had never thought she'd find somebody like that again. In some ways, he reminded her of Johnny with his quick wit and deep, gruff voice. In other ways, they were so different. Johnny had loved watching old westerns while Harry loved action movies. Johnny had been an early riser, often waking up before the sun, and he'd worked with his hands his whole life. Harry liked to sleep in on a lazy Sunday afternoon and wasn't the handiest person she'd ever met. But, he was a great cook and told the funniest jokes.

There were moments, especially early on, when she'd felt guilty about falling in love again. She knew that Johnny would want that for her, especially after she had waited so many years. He would never have wanted her to grow old alone.

At the same time, it had felt like she was betraying him, like she was saying that their years together hadn't mattered. It had been a real struggle, and one that she had to deal with alone out on the road. But when Harry had proposed on a whim and they found themselves standing in front of a Las Vegas preacher, she had known without a doubt that she was doing the right thing.

"So, what's up?" she asked, as she sat down at the table, sliding a piece of pie and a cup of coffee over to her son.

"Aren't you having any?"

She shook her head and smiled. "Darlin', I ate so much junk food on that trip. I'm trying to pack myself full of vegetables before we leave in a few weeks."

"I'm going to miss you," he said, softly. It did her heart good to hear him say that. For so many years, they hadn't been in contact at all, and hearing him admit that he would miss her, even on a short trip, warmed her heart.

"Don't you worry. We won't be gone that long. Harry has some family up in Virginia, so I think we're just going to head up there for a few weeks this summer so I can get to know them. He has two nieces, and they have a whole passel of kids."

William smiled. "I'm sure they'll love you as much as everyone does."

"Let's hope so, because they ain't getting rid of me!"

"Where is Harry?"

"Oh, he had a follow up appointment with his neurologist today. Mine isn't until next week. Gotta go see how this whole Parkinson's thing is going, get our medications refilled. You know the drill." She always downplayed the disease, unwilling to let it define who she was or how she lived her life.

"And how are you feeling?" he asked, still restlessly moving his fingers.

"I'm feeling fine, son. But you look like you're about to come out of your skin. Tell me what's going on."

"Well, I'm about to make a life-changing decision, and I just thought maybe I needed to talk to somebody about it first."

Dixie grinned. "Are you going to ask Janine to marry you?"

William almost choked on his coffee, putting it on the table and covering his mouth. "What would make you say that?"

"I don't know, just seemed like that's where you were headed. Don't you love her?"

"I do. But I don't think we're quite ready for that yet. Janine is still building her business, and I..."

"Spit it out, William. What's got you so rattled?"

"I'm a little afraid I'm going to disappoint you."

She stared at him. "Disappoint me? You could never do that. What on earth is going on?"

"You know I just started my own marketing firm after I came back from Texas, right?"

She nodded. "Of course. Janine told me you've been working morning, noon and night trying to make it successful. I'm proud of you for that."

"I'm thinking of closing it down."

Dixie's head jolted back a bit, her eyebrows knitted together in confusion. "Close it down? Have you given it enough time?"

He sighed. "I hate it, Mom. I loathe it with a passion. It's just what I thought I was good at, but I can't imagine getting up every morning for the rest of my life and running that business."

She reached over and rubbed his hand. "Well, then do something else."

He laughed. "You and Janine make everything sound so simple."

"Well, that's because it is simple. There's no need for a person to hate what they do. I wouldn't get up every day and run that bookstore if I didn't love it. Janine wouldn't do her yoga if she didn't love it. You need a passion, or you'll make yourself miserable."

"But I have rent to pay. And I need to be putting away for the future because I would like to marry Janine one day. But right now, I just feel like a big failure."

She squeezed his hand and looked him in the eye. "The only time you're a failure is if you quit. You're not quitting, are you? I mean, you're gonna find something else you like to do?"

He sucked in a deep breath and then blew it out. "Well, that's why I'm here. I sort of have something in mind."

She smiled. "See? I knew my William would have a back up plan. What is it?"

"I think I want to start a fishing business, in the marsh."

Now, she really was confused. "A fishing business? Like where you sell fish that you catch?"

William let out a laugh. "No. Like where I take people on trips. Teach them about the marsh, help them learn how to fish there. Work with tourists and locals."

"So, a fishing charter business?"

"Right. Janine had me do this silly exercise where she was trying to tap into my subconscious mind..."

Dixie held up her hand. "Lord, I don't understand what that girl is talking about sometimes."

He laughed. "Me either, but this one actually seemed to make sense. She asked me some questions, I had to answer fast and when she asked me what I wanted to do, suddenly fishing popped out of my mouth. I don't even know where it came from."

Dixie squinted her eyes at him. "You and I both know where it came from."

William stood up and paced back-and-forth next to the table. "Daddy?"

"You know it. That was always Johnny's dream. He wanted to take that old fishing boat, and show everybody how to fish those marsh waters. But he got stuck doing his job, and he never got to live that dream."

"But it's crazy, Mom. I don't even know how much money I could possibly make doing something like that."

She stood up and walked over to him, putting her hands on his upper arms and looking up at him. He was tall, like his dad. "You'll never know unless you try. And I have faith in you, son. You always land on your feet."

"I have another question."

"What's that?"

"Can I have daddy's boat?"

She smiled. It'd been years since she thought about that old rickety boat. She kept it in a storage unit over near Charleston. Johnny had bought it intending to work on it, being that he was so good with his hands. But right after he purchased it, he'd started getting sick. She just couldn't bear to look at it, so she put it away, out of sight and out of mind.

"Of course you can. But, and pardon me for saying so, you're not exactly the mechanical type."

William nodded. "Don't worry. I'm going to ask Dawson to help me. Maybe even Tucker, since he invents all kinds of intricate toys. Maybe he can help me too."

She chuckled. "Well, it sounds like a wonderful group project. Let me go get you the key to the storage unit." As she started walking toward the desk where she kept the key in the drawer, she turned around. "William?"

"Yeah?"

"I want you to know that your daddy is smiling down from heaven right now. He'll be there helping you get that boat set right. Don't you worry."

~

Colleen was more nervous than she ever had been in her life. She had been working all day around Dawson's property, trying to get set up for the foster kids' camp. It started in just a few days, and it seemed like there was still so much left to do.

So far, they had gotten the old barn turned into a bunkhouse for the kids since the inn was full of guests most of the time. Amy, the head of children and family services locally, would be sending social workers to stay overnight and make sure that all of the kids were accounted for.

The final count had been right at fifteen children. She had to admit, she didn't have a whole lot of experience working with kids, although Tucker did. He was just a big kid at heart. His playful nature and willingness to listen was going to be a big help when the kids got there.

She was getting a little nervous, wanting to make sure that it was a wonderful event for the children. They weren't making any money on this, and at times she had questioned why they had offered that. But then she would think about these kids who had no parents, and she knew that she was doing the right thing. While she was certain some of them were in great foster homes, she was also very well aware of how broken the foster care system could be. For the days that the kids would be with them, she was going to do her best to make it a great experience in their lives.

Lucy, Dawson's resident chef and stand-in grandmother, had created a beautiful menu for the children. Filled with peanut butter and jelly sandwiches, macaroni and cheese and chicken pot pie, the kids would be well fed the whole time they were there. They had planned to have a big breakfast outside each morning before doing all kinds of physical activities throughout the day, including kayaking and playing on the beach. They would run three-legged races, bob for apples and even do a little fishing.

By far, Tucker was most looking forward to teaching them about toys and inventions and all of the things that he found the most interesting. His secret hope was that one of the kids would become a toy inventor, but Colleen told him not to pressure the children.

"What else do y'all need?" Dawson asked, as he walked up behind Colleen. She was sitting at the picnic table on the back deck overlooking the ocean, furiously writing on a pad of paper attached to her clipboard. She had recently gotten the names and ages of the kids, she was trying to make sure that all of the activities would work well for every child.

"Nothing right now. You've been a godsend, Dawson. I really appreciate all of your help. I know you're busy running the inn."

He smiled. "You're like my daughter, so you know I don't mind."

Colleen smiled.

"Oh, I hope I didn't speak out of turn. I know you have a father..."

She laughed. "I don't mind at all, Dawson. I kind of think of you like a stepfather. Who knows? Maybe one day you will be."

He shook his head. "I don't know about that. I don't think your momma is wanting to get married again."

Colleen waved her hand in the air. "Oh, what does she know? She had a tough couple of years, but she seems to be head over heels in love with you."

"What about you girls? What would you think if your mom got married again?"

"We would be ecstatic. She deserves a second chance at love, and we wouldn't want anyone else in our family but you."

Dawson chuckled. "Well, maybe you can tell her that."

"Y'all aren't over here talking about me, are you?" Julie asked as she walked over. Colleen hadn't even noticed that she had parked her car just a few feet away.

"No, Mom. We have more things to talk about than you. How conceited," Colleen said jokingly as she rolled her eyes. Julie sat down beside her.

"Don't be sassy. What are you up to?"

Dawson leaned over the table and gave her a quick peck on the lips. "Your daughter has been amazing setting up this camp."

"Don't forget Tucker," Colleen said. Even though he had helped a lot, he was back at work on a conference call about a new toy they would be unveiling over the summer. Some mixture between a robot and a ghost. Colleen rarely understood what he was talking about, but she loved working with him anyway.

"Is there anything I can do to help?" Julie asked.

"Well, if you can help me organize all of these games by age group. I received the final list of kids, but I want to make sure that none of these games is too hard for the little ones or too easy for the big ones."

Julie took the clipboard and started looking it over. "I'll be happy to. Meg has a night class, so I don't have to get Vivi for a couple of hours."

"Where is Christian?"

"He's got some staff meetings this evening. So, of course, I offered to keep Vivi. I never miss an opportunity to squeeze those little cheeks," Julie said, laughing.

"I love watching you be a grandmother. I wish I could've watched you be a new mother," Dawson said, offhandedly.

"Me too," Julie said, softly. Colleen suddenly felt like she was sitting in the middle of a conversation where she didn't belong.

She loved her father, although sometimes he made it difficult. But, there were times that she looked at her mother and Dawson and wished they could've had more years together. Dawson would've made the best father she could imagine. He was protective, kind and fun. Some kid would've really benefited from having him as a dad. It made her sad to think that he lost his only child and would never get that chance again.

"Well, I'll leave you ladies to it. Colleen, if you need anything, I'll be out back. I'm building a new table for the breakfast room."

"I'll come back and see you in a minute," Julie said, smiling at him as he walked away.

"You guys are too cute," Colleen said, giggling. Julie bumped her shoulder.

"Stop it."

"You know he wants to marry you, right?"

Julie froze in place and then looked at her daughter. "Did he say that?"

"Not in so many words. But, I think that he thinks you wouldn't marry him."

Julie sighed. "It's not that. I just don't know if I'm ready for that, or if I'll ever be. No offense to your father, but that whole thing really took it out of me. I couldn't go through that again."

"He's not daddy. Dawson would never hurt you like that."

"I know. Let's not talk about it right now. Besides, I have a secret plan I need to run by you."

"What do you mean?"

"What if we throw a big wedding reception for Dixie and Harry? We could do it at my house or even here at the inn once the camp is over."

"That's a great idea! But, you're going to have to plan that one. I'm all planned out after this camp," Colleen said, putting her head down on the table. Julie patted her on the back.

"Oh, I've got big plans."

CHAPTER FIVE

Meg took a bite of her sandwich and stared off into the distance. Vivi was finally down for the night, and it had been a long one. Her mother had kept her until class was over, and then Meg had gone to pick her up. She went home, fed her dinner and waited for Christian to get back from work. When he finally did, it took them hours to get Vivi to sleep. She wasn't sure, but she had a feeling that her mother had given her chocolate ice cream because she had seen the empty carton in the kitchen. Either that, or her mother had a really big sweet tooth.

"You look exhausted," Christian said as he walked into the kitchen. He sat down beside her, rubbing her arm.

"I am exhausted. Between school and being a mom, I'm starting to feel a little bit like a failure. Or a zombie. Or maybe a zombie failure."

Christian chuckled. "You're doing fine. It's hard, and even harder for you. I get to be at work all day, and I know you're struggling with keeping up with your schoolwork and taking care of Vivi. But it's all going to pay off."

"I know. And I love my daughter more than anything

in this world. I wouldn't trade this life for any amount of money."

Christian leaned over and kissed her. Lately, that was kind of rare, not because he wasn't romantic. He was French, after all. But their time together was limited, usually reserved for late nights when Vivi was either still awake or they were both too tired to even bother with hugs or kisses or anything else.

"I want to ask you something," Christian said. He seemed a little nervous, and she couldn't imagine why.

"What?"

"Have you thought anymore about what we talked about a few days ago?"

"You mean getting married?"

"Yes. It's all I've thought about all week."

She smiled and rubbed her thumb across his cheek. "You're so romantic."

"I try. I want us to get married, Meg. Make it official."

"I know. And I want that too. But, right now I couldn't possibly enjoy planning a wedding and all of that."

"Then we can go to the justice of the peace."

She stared at him. "Christian, I'm only going to get married one time in my life, and I don't want it to be in front of the justice of the peace."

"I know, my love. I'm sorry. I just want to be able to tell people that you're my wife."

"And I want people to know that you're my husband. I realize we did this whole thing out of the traditional order, having a baby first. But I want a special wedding day. I want to do all of the planning with my sister and my mother. I want to pick a dress, a venue, taste test all of the wedding cakes I can get my hands on..."

Christian smiled. "You're right. All of that is important."

"Right now, I can't even keep my head on straight between math class and teething. I couldn't possibly enjoy the process of planning a wedding."

"Then we will wait. When you feel ready, I am here. Always willing. You say the word."

She leaned up and kissed him on the cheek. "I promise that I will marry you. Just let me get through these next few months of school, and then we'll start planning. And we will have the most magical day any two people could ever have."

~

SuAnn rolled out the dough for the umpteenth time. No matter how many times she followed the recipe, she couldn't seem to get it just perfect. Although the pie tasted divine, it had to look perfect, like something out of a magazine. She was determined to beat Henrietta Bankston if it was the last thing she did.

"How many more times are you going to bake this pie?" Darcy asked as she walked out of the back room with more cupcakes from the fridge.

"As many times as it takes, I suppose." She continued staring down at the dough as she carved the thin slices of it to lay over the top in a lattice design.

"What's the big deal about this contest anyway?" Darcy asked as she pulled herself up onto the counter.

"I told you to quit sitting up there. You're not a child," SuAnn scolded. Begrudgingly, Darcy jumped down and leaned against the counter, her arms crossed.

"Fine, *Mom*," she said, sarcastically. SuAnn still wasn't

sure she liked Darcy all that much, but she gave as good as she got and was okay with the customers for the most part.

"If I was your mom, I'd teach you better manners," SuAnn said, looking back down at the dough.

"Is there big prize money or something?"

SuAnn looked up. "You know, I have no idea."

Darcy chuckled. "Then why all this fuss?"

"Have you ever had an arch nemesis?"

"An arch nemesis? Like in superhero movies?"

SuAnn shrugged her shoulders. "I don't know anything about superheroes. I mean someone who just gets under your skin like a piece of fiberglass insulation and makes you want to rip off your own flesh?"

Darcy shook her head. "You really have a vivid imagination."

"Surely you have someone who just rubs you the wrong way?"

She nodded. "There was this girl in high school - Elaine Draper. Yuck. She was the senior class president, homecoming queen and every guy's dream girl. I couldn't stand her. She was so stuck up, and everything came so easy for her. She started a rumor about me that I stole money from a teacher's purse, which I didn't do. I ended up getting suspended from school for the rest of the semester."

"Wow. Then you get it. Henrietta Bankston is my arch nemesis."

"Bankston... why does that sound familiar?"

"She's the mayor's wife."

"Oh, that's right. So your arch nemesis is the mayor's wife? Did you get into a fight with her or something?"

"Not exactly. She came in here and was very snotty. I

didn't like it." She looked back down at the dough and groaned under her breath, wadding it up into a ball again.

"So you just didn't like the way she talked to you? And now you want to rip your own skin off?"

"It might sound ridiculous to you, but I don't like being patronized. She thinks she can win this thing, and I'm going to prove her wrong."

"Does the lady even really care about winning?"

SuAnn stared at her. "She's won the last twelve years in a row."

Darcy's mouth dropped open. "Yikes. I don't like your chances."

"You don't know me all that well yet. But, I always get what I want."

Darcy laughed. "I can see that. Well, for what it's worth, I hope you beat old Henrietta Bankston. And I hope there's big prize money in it for you."

"Thanks, dear."

Darcy walked across the room to wipe down one of the tables. "And just so you know, I got my revenge on Elaine Draper."

SuAnn looked up. "Oh yeah? What did you do?"

"She had this beautiful long hair. Everybody wanted her hair. I may or may not have hidden behind her in the movie theater with a big wad of gum. It was so bad, she had to cut a bunch off," she said, scrunching her nose.

"You've got to be kidding! You made that poor girl cut her hair?"

Darcy couldn't help but chuckle. "Maybe. She had to cut it really short and looked like a boy at prom. It wasn't pretty. Here she was with her long, flowing pink gown and a super short haircut that looked like she was entering military service."

"That's terrible!" SuAnn, waving her hand at Darcy as she tried not to laugh. "But I might need your advice on a few things if I can't get this pie to work. Keep that gum handy. Hen has a big bouffant hairdo."

Darcy nodded and grinned. "I have a few tricks up my sleeve, for sure. You just say the word."

SuAnn rolled her eyes, but secretly wondered if she might need Darcy's help after all. It sounded like she was a much better friend than an enemy.

~

"Come on! Let me do this for you. We're long overdue for a big party anyway!" Julie said. Dixie rolled her eyes.

"You just love planning shindigs, don't you?"

Julie smiled. "If it's for my best friend in the world, yes. We need to celebrate your new marriage!"

"Honey, you don't have to go to all that trouble. I love you for offering..."

"It's no trouble. We'll do it at the inn two weeks from Sunday. That will give Dawson time to get things back in order after the foster kids' camp. Sound good?"

Dixie shrugged her shoulders and laughed. "Works for me. I just don't want to be a bother."

Julie put her hands on Dixie's shoulders. "You've done so much for everyone in this community. Let us be excited and celebrate your new adventure, okay?"

"Fine. Okay. But, please don't spend a bunch of money. I'm not royalty or anything."

"Well, you're *our* royalty around here. How's Harry?" Julie asked as she wiped down the counter where they served coffee. A customer had spilled more sugar than they'd used.

"He's much better. The doc says his ankle is all healed up, and he's currently down at the storage unit with William. They're assessing what the boat needs. Harry has some experience in that area."

"That's great. Janine told me what William is planning. I never would've expected that."

Dixie sat down at the bistro table with a cup of coffee. "Yeah, me neither. His daddy was big into fishing and boating, but William never seemed like the type to go into it as a career. Don't get me wrong, I'm proud of him for trying something new. I sure hope it works out. He's had a heck of a time finding his place in the world."

Julie took the used coffee filter out of the machine and dropped it into the trash can before replacing it and starting the machine again. "Yeah, I understand that myself. I still don't know what I want to do when I grow up."

Dixie laughed. "Life is all about endings and beginnings. As long as you don't get stuck on an ending, you'll do fine."

Julie sat down. "Maybe I am stuck on an ending."

"You mean Michael?"

Julie nodded. "Where do I go from here? I just work, play with my grandbaby and date Dawson?"

Dixie looked at her questioningly. "Do you want more?"

"Don't we all?"

"Sugar, do you want to marry Dawson?"

Julie sighed. "I don't know. I said I never wanted to get married again. But, I don't know if I truly meant it. I meant it at the time I said it..."

Dixie reached over and squeezed her hand. "Julie, it's

okay to change your mind. Dawson loves you, and I know he wants a future with you."

"We're in a good place right now. There's no need to rush things."

"Are you saying that because you think it's the right thing to say or because you actually feel that way?"

"I have no idea."

"Do you want to date other people?"

Julie stared at Dixie. She had never even considered that idea, actually. It wasn't like she got divorced so she could play the field. Her plan had been to stay married to Michael forever, although she was happy that those prayers hadn't been answered favorably.

"Absolutely not. Dawson is perfect for me. If things don't work out with him, I've lost all hope in love." She wasn't joking. Her relationship with Dawson was everything she'd ever dreamed of. All of those years with Michael, she'd thought she had a good marriage. Not perfect, but livable. Adequate. Looking back, she'd been settling for at least the last ten years of their marriage. There was no settling with Dawson. He was a good partner, a wonderful friend and a strong, steady presence in her life.

"Honey, I believe you're overthinking this whole thing. Look, I said I'd never get married again and now I'm sitting here with a big old gold band on my finger. When love comes along and knocks you right over the head, you can't help but believe in second chances."

Julie smiled. "I'm so happy for you and Harry."

"Don't change the subject. The question remains - would you marry Dawson if he asked?"

"I..."

The doorbell chimed just in time to stop Julie from

having to answer that question. Miss Bessie, her favorite customer, was being wheeled in by her caregiver.

"Hey there, old lady," Bessie joked when she saw Dixie. "Where've you been?"

Dixie stood up and walked over to hug her. "Oh, I've just been doing some traveling with my new husband."

Bessie's eyes widened. "You went and got married? You crazy old bat!"

The two women had been friends for ages, and Julie loved to hear them rib each other. "I know, I know. But, he's a good man. You'll like him."

"Oh, you know I'm happy for you, old friend," Bessie said, squeezing Dixie's hand.

"Maybe your Prince Charming is out there?" Dixie teased.

"Yeah, well, he can stay out there. I'm too old to put up with any man's crap!"

Julie couldn't help but laugh at their conversation. She imagined that she and Janine might have a similar conversation when they aged a few more decades.

"Hey there, pretty lady," she said as Julie walked over and rubbed her shoulder.

"Good afternoon, Miss Bessie."

"Tell me something good." She would always ask this when she saw Julie. It was her "thing". She said hearing one good thing each day made for a beautiful, happy life. Julie believed her.

Julie sat back down at the table, as did Dixie. "Well, I'm throwing this wonderful woman a big wedding reception in a couple of weeks, and I think that's pretty dang good! And you're invited, Miss Bessie. You as well, Amelia," she said to her caregiver. Amelia smiled.

"Oh, I don't get out much to parties these days, but that sure is a good thing!"

"What about you, Miss Bessie? What's your good thing today?"

She smiled slightly. "Well, darlin', I found out this morning that my grandson is coming to get me."

"I'm not sure I understand?"

"My grandson, Carl, lives in Tampa. He just retired from being a police officer, and he and his wife are coming to take me to live with them."

Julie was stunned and a little heartsick. She knew what this meant. Once Bessie left Seagrove, the likelihood of ever seeing her again was minimal. She was in her nineties, after all.

"Oh, wow. Are you happy to be leaving? You grew up here, didn't you?" Julie asked.

"I sure did. Man, I ran around on these beaches my whole life. Raised my kids here too. But, life takes funny twists and turns sometimes, doesn't it?"

Dixie smiled. "I sure will miss you."

Bessie reached out and held her hand. "Honey, I know where I'm going one day, and I know I'll see you both there."

"Let's not talk about things like that," Julie pleaded, her eyes welling with tears.

"Dying's all a part of living, honey. Live while you're young! Do all the things you want to do, especially the ones that scare you half to death!"

Something about what she said resonated deep in Julie's heart. She literally felt it go through her, like someone had hit her in the chest with a heavy book.

"When do you leave?" Dixie asked.

"End of the week. He's got a whole apartment set up for me. Amelia's coming too!"

Julie looked at Amelia. She'd been taking care of Bessie for years, according to Dixie. "Are you excited?"

"I am. I couldn't bear to leave Miss Bessie's side. We've been together a long time," she said. Amelia was getting up in age herself, but she was devoted to Bessie. It was heartwarming to see. Julie imagined Carl would end up caring for Amelia at some point too.

"So this is your last visit to our little bookstore?" Julie asked.

Bessie nodded sadly. "I'm afraid so, but I sure will think about y'all every time I get Amelia to read me a book."

"Well, what kind of book are you looking for today then?" Dixie asked.

"I'd like to get some books about Florida. I need to know all about my new home state," she said, smiling broadly.

"I think we can help you with that!" Dixie waved her hand, and Amelia followed, pushing Bessie in the wheelchair. As Julie watched them go to the back of the store, it occurred to her just how quickly life could change.

One minute, you think you're happily married, and your husband comes home and destroys everything.

One minute, your daughter is a college student in France, and the next minute she's a mother.

One minute, your favorite customer is sitting in front of you, and the next she's moving to Tampa, and you'll likely never see her again.

Julie sighed. Life sure could turn on a dime.

CHAPTER SIX

William stood back and looked at the boat. Even though he, Dawson and Harry had been working on it for a couple of weeks now, it still looked like a wreck, at least cosmetically.

Thankfully, Harry had been able to fix a lot of the mechanical issues. It was definitely seaworthy now, and Tucker had been by a couple of times to help as well. The foster kids' camp was taking up much of his time, which William totally understood.

"I don't think people are going to want to get on this boat with the way that it looks. Personally, I would assume it would sink before we even got away from the dock," William said. Dawson, the only person helping him today, laughed.

"Which is why we're going to start painting it. Of course, we need to start sanding first. And you might want to consider replacing the flooring. I'm not sure there's much we can do with this."

William looked down at the warped wooden floors, holes sporadically scattered across the surface. "You don't think we could put a big piece of plexiglass and just say that it's one of those cool glass bottom boats?"

Dawson chuckled. "Yeah, I'm gonna say no on that one."

"I didn't realize how much work this thing was going to take. Are you hungry?"

"Starving. I worked all morning helping to set up for the camp, so honestly this was a nice break. Colleen is quite the dictator," he said, sitting down on the dock and hanging his legs over the side. "She was getting a little stressed out this morning. I've never heard her raise her voice, so I got the heck out of dodge."

William pulled a cooler out of the boat and joined him, sitting down and putting it in his lap. He reached in and removed a couple of sandwiches, handing one to Dawson.

"When I went by to see Janine this morning, Julie gave me these. She said they were your favorite," William said, in a singsongy way.

Dawson bumped William's shoulder with his. "Don't be jealous. At least my girlfriend knows how to cook."

William laughed. "Well, you've got me there. Janine's great at heating up macaroni and cheese and the occasional cold pizza, but she's certainly no chef."

"But you love her."

He nodded. "That I do. The fact that she's okay with me starting up this new venture and doesn't think I'm some sort of immature, adolescent boy is amazing."

"Yeah, I guess we're both lucky that way. We found two women who want us to dream big and do what we love. Not many of them out there."

William took a bite of his sandwich. "I don't know how Julie makes these taste so much better than regular sandwiches."

Dawson nodded. "I know, right? She's a sandwich magician."

They sat there for a few minutes, devouring the sandwiches and potato chips that Julie had sent along. When they were finished, they each leaned back with their hands on the dock, staring up into the sky. "How are we supposed to work now? I feel like I'm about to pop!" Dawson said, putting his hand on his stomach and rubbing it.

"I guess we better sit for a little bit and let our food settle."

"I suppose so."

"I'm really glad you're doing this. I know your father would be so thrilled right now."

"I sure wish he could be here," William said. "There's not a day that goes by that I don't miss that man. He knew the answer for everything. I'm so afraid I'm going to screw this whole thing up."

"Listen, I was scared of that when I started my contracting business. I was scared of that when I started the inn. A little healthy fear never hurt anybody."

"I just don't wanna look like a fool. The last thing I want is for Janine to look at me at some point and know that I'm a failure."

Dawson slapped him on the back. "Stop thinking like that, man! This thing's going to be successful. All businesses start off a little bit shaky, but when you do what you love every day, that really comes through."

"I guess so. It's just really different going from being in an office, wearing a suit all day to this," he said, laughing as he looked down at his khaki shorts, bare feet and paint stained T-shirt.

"Well, I told you not to start painting that railing before we sanded. What were you thinking?"

William laughed. "This isn't exactly my forte, which is why I asked you to come over here."

Dawson stood up and stretched his arms high above his head. "Look, you have friends and family that will be here for you. You don't have to do this alone. We take care of each other, and I'll be sure to tell everybody who visits my inn to come take one of your charter trips."

William stood up and shook his hand. "I appreciate your support."

"Now you sound like a politician," Dawson said, laughing. "Come on, let's get started on that sanding."

They climbed back into the boat, each of them picking up a piece of sandpaper. As they started working on the railings, they continued talking about life.

"So, do you think you'll marry Julie?"

Dawson stopped and looked at him. "Did Janine tell you to ask me that?"

"No. We have never talked about it, actually. It just seems like the next logical step."

"Well if it's the next logical step, are you going to marry Janine?"

"I hope so. One day. But, first I need to make this successful. I just can't go into a marriage without being able to support my family."

"I get that."

"Don't dodge the question. Are you going to propose to Julie?"

Dawson shrugged his shoulders. "I would marry Julie in a heartbeat. The problem is, I don't think she feels the same."

"Are you kidding me? That woman is head over heels for you!"

Dawson stopped sanding and leaned against the rail. "Maybe so, but there's a difference between wanting to date somebody and wanting to marry them. The few, very brief conversations that we've had about this topic, Julie has made it pretty clear that she doesn't want to get married again."

"How long ago did she say that?"

"I don't know. A few months ago, I guess."

"Maybe she's changed her mind. A lot of time has passed. She went through a really nasty divorce, so I'm sure it takes a lot of time to get over that."

"I know. Which is why I haven't pushed. But I have to say, I kind of feel like I'm in this holding pattern. I'm a marriage kind of guy. I want her living under the same roof with me. I want to think of Meg's daughter as my granddaughter. There's just so much more with marriage."

William stopped sanding and leaned against the opposite railing. "Are you afraid you're wasting your time dating her? I mean, what if she never wants to get married?"

Dawson sighed. "I don't know what I'll do. I certainly don't want to be with anyone else, but I also don't want to spend the rest of my life with a girlfriend. I want a wife. I'm just not sure I'm able to get that with Julie."

"Then maybe you should talk to her, man. Fear lives in the dark. Just bring it out in the light. Lay it all out and see what happens."

Dawson chuckled. "Look at you being a philosopher," he said, tossing the piece of sandpaper at William and hitting him right in the forehead.

William laughed and shrugged his shoulders. "I date a yoga teacher. What else do you expect from me?"

~

Colleen was a nervous wreck. As she watched the kids file off the small passenger van, she wondered what in the world she'd gotten herself into. She knew next to nothing about kids, especially ones that had been traumatized in some way. Maybe this was more than she was capable of handling.

She took in a deep breath, like her aunt Janine had advised her to do when she was under stress, and remembered that she wasn't alone. Tucker was standing right beside her, and Dawson was on the other side. Together, the three of them were determined to make this an amazing event for these kids.

She had always been the type to take on immense amounts of responsibility. Even when something didn't require that, she always felt like things were her fault and rested on her shoulders. Sometimes it served her well, especially in work environments. But, other times it put her in a situation of being way too hard on herself.

"Wow, there's more of them than I thought. Are we sure it's only fifteen kids?" Tucker said quietly.

Amy, the head of the foster care office, walked over to them, a big smile on her face. The kids were still lined up next to the bus with a couple of social workers.

"I promise that it's just fifteen kids," she said. "You guys look a little rattled."

Colleen managed to smile. "We're just exhausted. I had no idea how much work went into setting up a camp, so I really hope the kids enjoy it."

"They're super excited. They've never been involved in anything like this, so I'm sure they're going to love it. Should we head over to the bunks?"

Colleen and Dawson had managed to get some local furniture stores to donate bunkbeds for the barn. It wasn't an old, rickety barn. It was pretty state of the art, Dawson having only built it a couple of years ago. It also had its own HVAC system which meant that the kids would be perfectly comfortable out there. Dawson had actually built it with the idea of being able to rent it out for weddings, even before he'd decided to open the inn.

"Absolutely. Why don't we walk over and meet the kids, and we will show them where they're staying."

The three of them followed Amy over to the bus. The kids were squirmy and full of energy. At least, most of them were. There were a couple that looked shell-shocked and honestly didn't look like they wanted to be there.

"Kids, these are your hosts for the camp. I'm going to let them introduce themselves to you."

Taken aback, Colleen decided she probably should be first given that Tucker looked like he wanted to run away. He wasn't the greatest in situations where he had to be the center of attention.

"Well, my name is Colleen. And this is my coworker, Tucker. We work for a toy invention company, and we're super excited to show you guys some of our inventions and help you come up with some of your own."

The kids just stood there, staring at her, blankly. She realized what she had just described probably sounded a lot like school, and these kids definitely weren't interested in school right now.

"Hi, guys. My name is Tucker. As Colleen said, we work for a toy invention company, we have some really cool things to show you guys. We will be having some classes later in the week. You can draw your own inventions, and we'll talk about some of our more successful ones."

Again, she could swear that she heard crickets even over the ocean waves behind her. This was not going well.

"Hey, kids! I'm Dawson. I own this beautiful inn behind us. And we're gonna have tons of fun this week. We're going to do some fishing, playing in the ocean, do some fun outdoor games. We're going to eat some amazing food, and there will be all kinds of prizes!"

The kids let out a big roar, some of them clapping and laughing. Colleen looked at him, thankful that Dawson had gotten them excited.

"What prizes?" Colleen whispered in Dawson's ear.

He shrugged his shoulders. "I don't know. We'll figure it out." She couldn't help but laugh.

"Colleen, why don't you show us where the kids will be staying?" Amy said.

Colleen nodded and waved for everyone to follow her. Dawson followed along closely while Tucker stayed back, probably thankful to get out of the situation for a few minutes.

"So this is the bunkhouse..."

"This looks like a barn!" a young boy shouted out. He looked to be about eight or nine years old, scruffy brown hair, freckles across his nose and a huge gap between his teeth. He was adorable but looked like a throwback from the 1950s. She expected he was the type of little boy that liked to hang out in the creek beds, looking for worms and muscadines.

"Well, it is a barn..."

"Gross. We're staying in a barn? We're not animals!" a little girl shouted out.

"Actually, it's very nice..."

The kids couldn't hear Colleen over their very loud whining. She wasn't sure she would ever have children after this.

"Hey, kids, listen up!" Dawson said, his voice commanding. The kids all stopped talking and looked up at him. "I built this place with my bare hands. It's the nicest barn you're ever going to see in your lives complete with brand new bunkbeds. Now, I can get the tents out of my garage and we can do a camp out, or you can check this place out and see what you think. Is that a deal?"

"I don't want to sleep in a tent! I'm scared of bugs!" the same little girl said.

"Then why don't we check this place out first?"

The kids nodded as Dawson walked over and slid the barn doors open. Colleen could hear the kids gasp when they saw what a nice place it was. With soaring beams and beautiful chandelier style light fixtures hanging from the ceiling, it was no barn. It might've looked that way on the outside, but no animals were ever getting in here.

The kids started running around, tossing their bags onto whichever bed they were choosing. Colleen let out a sigh of relief as she turned to Dawson. "Thank you so much for taking control. I didn't know what to say to these little rugrats."

Dawson laughed. "I guess I'm good with kids because I have a very immature brain." She slapped him on the arm lightly.

"No, you don't. But you are good with them. It's a shame that..." Before she could stop herself, the words had just popped right out of her mouth. Knowing that Dawson had lost his only child, she couldn't believe she had stuck her foot in her mouth so badly. "Oh my gosh, Dawson. I'm so sorry. I didn't mean to say that..."

He smiled. "It's okay, Colleen. I know what you meant. It is a shame. I feel like I would've been a pretty good dad. I guess I won't ever know."

The sadness that washed over her almost made her cry. She loved her own father, of course. But she would've been happy to have a father like Dawson, and she wished there was a way he could experience that. But for now, she had to focus on the camp. There were fifteen little crazy people running around the barn, and she had to reassess whether she knew what in the world to do to keep them all entertained for the next week.

~

Dawson leaned back against the heavy Adirondack chair and blew out a long breath. He was exhausted. Absolutely fatigued all the way to his core in a way he'd never felt in his life. Kids took a lot of work!

Now that it was night time, he appreciated a few minutes of solitude. The only thing he could hear, besides the distant giggling in the bunkhouse, was the ocean waves in front of him. He loved having a deck right beside the ocean. No place on earth felt more peaceful to him.

"Glass of wine?" Julie said from behind him. He hadn't even heard her pull up.

"You know I'm not a wine guy," he said with a chuckle.

Julie walked closer and put a can of beer in front of his face. "Yes, I know that." She sat down in the chair next to him, reaching over and rubbing his arm. "Long day?"

"Extremely. Those kids are so full of energy. It was actually a lot of fun."

"I'm glad you had a good time. Lucy said they ate way

more food than she thought they would so she's going to have to cook more tomorrow."

"Yeah, we didn't have nearly enough. Some of those boys eat twice what I do in a day!"

"I never had boys, so I wouldn't know, but my girls ate a lot. Constant snacking, as I remember."

He took a sip of his beer. "It was fun. We did a bunch of competitions, gave away some prizes. Colleen and I weren't exactly prepared for that, so she snuck away in the middle of the day to get a few things. It's amazing what kids will do for a pack of gum or a stuffed animal."

Julie laughed. "Well, it sounds like you had an eventful day. I kept Vivi for a little while, worked at the bookstore. Finally wrote another scene for my novel."

He looked over at her and smiled. She was so beautiful. She just had that girl next-door look that every guy dreamed of. And she really was like that, so down to earth, funny and kind. Like his perfect partner sent straight from heaven. He flashed back to his conversation with William and wondered if she would ever be interested in marriage again.

"I miss you," he said. She looked at him, her eyebrows furrowed together.

"I'm sitting right here."

He reached over and squeezed her hand. Sitting there with her, in two big Adirondack chairs overlooking the ocean, was the best place he could imagine on earth. When he let his mind run away with itself, he could imagine them sitting in those very same chairs watching grandchildren run around and play on the sand. "I mean I miss that we don't get to spend so much time together these days. I'm busy with the inn, and then this camp.

You're busy with work and that new grand baby. Everything just feels like it gets more complicated by the day."

Julie put down her wine glass and stood up. She took his can and put it on the table before sliding down into his lap and laying her head against his chest. Now he really was in his favorite place on earth.

"I'm always here. I'm not going anywhere."

"I know, but I guess..."

He hesitated on saying anything further. The last thing he needed, especially after such a long day, was a deep emotional conversation. His brain just couldn't take much more.

"But what?" She pulled back and looked at him, concern written all over her face.

He rubbed his thumb over her cheek. "I guess I just wish that at the end of *every* long day, you were here, waiting for me."

"But I am here. And I can come by more often, every day if you want."

Dawson shook his head. "You're not really understanding what I'm saying. I mean that I would love it if we turned out the lights together every night and went upstairs to our own room."

Julie sat back and stared at him, her face unreadable. "Dawson, I guess I'm old-school but I just don't believe in living together. I mean, I know Meg and Christian are living together but that's a little bit different because they have a child..."

He chuckled. "I'm not asking you to live with me, Julie. I'm just wishing and hoping."

"Hoping for what exactly?"

He sighed. "You know what? This is great. We have the

perfect set up. I guess I'm just a little tired tonight and overthinking things."

"Are you sure?"

He smiled and kissed her hand. "I'm sure. I'm one lucky man, and I will never take that for granted."

Julie laid her head back down on his chest. As he ran his hand over her hair, he wished he had the courage to say what he really wanted to say. Maybe he should've proposed in that moment. Maybe he should've just thrown it all out there like William recommended. The fear got to him. The fear that she would say no. The fear that she would walk away. The fear that nothing would ever be the same again. For tonight, he was content to just hold her in his arms and wish for the future of his dreams.

CHAPTER SEVEN

Julie sat at the table across from Janine and Meg. Getting away for a quick lunch to start planning Dixie and Harry's reception was a wonderful break in her day. Christian was keeping the baby so that the girls could go out to lunch. Of course, Colleen was way too busy running the camp back at the inn.

"So, I think that eight tables should be enough. We should be able to seat at least six people at each. I've also been working on the guest list. I don't think Dixie wants it to be a huge affair," Julie said, sliding a diagram across the table to her sister and daughter. It was good to have people helping her plan, because this whole thing could easily have been overwhelming for one person to handle.

"How are we set on the food? I know you were going to have the bistro do the catering?"

"Yes. And we're also going to have a food truck there. They're going to be doing desserts and margaritas."

"You found a food truck that does desserts and margaritas? And why can't we hire them full-time to just sit outside of your house?" Meg asked, laughing.

"First off, you're underage, young lady. And secondly, they're bookstore customers, so they're doing me a favor. They normally sell barbecue."

Janine laughed. "I don't think Dixie would be okay with barbecue at her wedding reception, so good plan on the desserts and drinks."

"Dawson said that we can use this area over here for the dance floor," Julie said, pointing to her diagram.

"What about a DJ?" Janine asked.

"Already handled. I have to work with him on the music list because I highly doubt that Dixie is going to want rap music or the latest country crooner. I know she and Harry really enjoy big band and old jazz."

"Boring," Meg said under her breath. Of course, she was only a twenty year old. She certainly wasn't into big band music.

"That should about cover everything. If you guys can just help with some of the final details, we should be good to go. I thought it might be fun to have the pastor there and an archway with flowers so that Harry and Dixie can say their vows again in front of everyone. What do you think?"

"I think that will be beautiful," Janine said, smiling. "It's all so romantic. I mean, I know it's not a real wedding or anything, but it's the next best thing."

"Christian asked me the other day about getting married."

"What did you say?" Julie asked, hopeful that her daughter was ready to tie the knot. Her old fashioned values were coming out again, but she really wanted to see a wedding ring on her daughter's finger now that she and Christian had a child together.

"I'm not ready yet. I want to finish up with my

schooling so that I can totally focus on a big, beautiful wedding. I know I want to marry Christian. I don't have any doubts about that, but I'm in no rush."

Julie felt a bit crestfallen by that, but she wasn't going to show it. The relationship she had with Meg was wonderful, and her daughter was an adult. She was a mother herself. She was perfectly capable of making her own life decisions whether Julie always agreed with them or not.

"I don't know if I would want a big wedding, but I'm a lot older than you," Janine said. "Of course, William and I are nowhere near getting married. We've had a few blips in our relationship, and he is so focused on his new business. We have a little ways to go before we get there."

"I'm with you on the big wedding thing. If I ever got married again, I would want a small ceremony, just a few friends and family. I did the whole big white dress, fancy ceremony. One time was enough."

Meg and Janine stared at Julie. "You're thinking about getting married again?" Meg asked.

"Oh, no. Besides, Dawson hasn't asked me."

Janine grinned. "What would you say if he did ask you?"

Julie rolled her eyes. "I don't play pretend, my dear sister."

"Oh, come on! You know you'd love to marry Dawson. He's the catch of the county!"

Julie laughed. "Don't tell him that. He'll get a big head."

"It's hard to imagine you being married again," Meg said. Julie couldn't read the look on her face.

"I'm not getting married. I was just talking about weddings because y'all were."

"But what would you say if he asked you?" Meg said.

"I don't know. I'm not sure I'd ever want to get married again. Dawson was talking kind of funny about it last night. He said he wished I was there every night so then we could turn off the lights at the end of the night and go to our own room."

"Gross," Meg said, pretending like she was about to throw up.

Julie laughed. "Well, that's what he said."

"He loves you so much, sis. You couldn't find a better man."

Julie looked at Meg, worried that Janine's comment might have offended her. After all, Michael was her father, and she didn't want anyone trying to ruin her daughters' relationship with their dad, no matter what a dirtbag he was.

"I don't have to make any decisions about this right now. Dawson hasn't even asked, and I don't know that he ever will. Things are great right now. Why rock the boat?"

Janine smiled and rubbed her sister's hand. "Don't let fear keep you from moving forward, Julie. You deserve happiness, and Dawson does too."

She wanted to believe that was true, that she'd finally met the man of her dreams, someone who would never hurt her. But, there was still a small part of her sending off warning bells. She'd thought Michael would never hurt her, and yet he did. In a big way. Betrayal was the hardest thing to get over, and she wasn't sure she could ever be that vulnerable again.

~

Dawson blew the whistle and all of the kids froze in place, each of them pretending to be a statue. He blew the whistle again and watched them run around like maniacs.

"This is fun. I wish I could control everyone in my life by blowing this whistle," he said to Colleen.

"Tell me about it. Are we ready to break for lunch?"

"Yeah, Lucy has it all ready over there on the tables. Mind grabbing a jug of sweet tea from the fridge?"

"Sure." Colleen walked off, and Dawson blew the whistle again.

"Hey, kids? Time to line up for lunch!"

As the kids walked down the side of the table, loading their plates with hamburgers and chips, Dawson settled himself under a big live oak tree and took a long drink of his water bottle. Today had been a hot one so far, and the kids were keeping him busy. But, he loved it.

"How tall are you?" a little boy suddenly asked. Dawson hadn't even seen him standing there. He knew the kid's name was Dylan and that he was eight years old, but that was about it.

"I'm six foot-one. Why?"

Dylan sat down next to Dawson, his plate teetering on his lap. "My daddy was taller than you."

"Oh yeah?"

"Yeah. But he died."

Dawson's breath caught in this throat. What was he supposed to say to that?

"I'm sorry to hear that. My daddy died too."

Dylan looked up at him, his emerald green eyes wide. "He did? How?"

"His heart just gave out."

"My daddy did something bad."

Dawson didn't know what to say. He didn't want to further traumatize the kid by asking questions.

"Looks like he also did something good when he made you."

"I guess so. But, nobody really wants me now."

"Dylan, that's not true. You've got Miss Amy, your friends here at camp and your foster family. And me."

He ate one of his chips and stared off in space. "I like this place. My foster mom has a small house. I don't get my own room. I share it with two other kids."

"You do?"

"Yeah. One of them isn't nice. He makes fun of my red hair and freckles."

"I think your red hair and freckles are super cool. I always wanted freckles."

Dylan looked up at him, one eyebrow raised. "Really?"

"Oh yeah. My friend, Billy, had these cool freckles all over his face. Even more than you. He was the most popular guy in my school."

"Because of the freckles?"

"Totally. I mean, everybody knows that freckles are only given to the strongest people. God does that so we all know who those people are."

"Are you sure?" Dylan asked, soaking up everything Dawson said.

"Absolutely. I wish I could have freckles. It's one of my life regrets that I don't." He had no idea what he was saying to the kid, but it seemed to be going over well.

Dylan leaned back against the tree and took a bite of his sandwich. "I never knew my mom."

Yikes. This kid was deep. Dawson didn't feel at all prepared for this. "I'm sorry you didn't get to know her."

"She left when I was a baby. I guess she didn't want me because she never came back."

Sometimes, there were no words.

~

Janine sat at the bistro table, sipping on her iced coffee and eating a bowl of French onion soup. It was a weird combination, but she didn't care. Having a quiet lunch alone was just what she needed today.

Between the planning for Dixie's wedding reception and William frantically trying to get his business up and running, her brain was a bit frazzled lately. She had taught two yoga classes that morning, and she just wanted a few moments of peace. Which was another reason why she had opted to eat lunch across the square and away from her mother's bakery. If she sat anywhere nearby, SuAnn would always find her and talk her ear off. She loved her mother, but sometimes she just needed the peace.

SuAnn was feverishly preparing for the pie baking contest that was coming up in a couple of days, and it was like she'd had a few hundred espressos. Her level of enthusiasm over pie baffled Janine.

"Oh, hey, Janine." She looked up to see Dawson standing there. She had been so lost in thought that she hadn't even seen him walk up.

"Hey there. Oh, man, you look tired."

Dawson pointed to the chair across from her. "Mind if I sit down for a minute?"

She nodded. Dawson was never a bother. "Sure, go ahead."

"I don't usually see you over on this side of the square."

"It's been a long couple of days, so I just needed some

peace. Plus, my mother can't find me over here when I sit behind this fountain."

Dawson laughed. "And here I am interrupting your peaceful lunch. I'm sorry. I can go..."

"No! You stay put. Plus, I know my week hasn't been nearly as eventful as yours."

"Yeah, it's been a little crazy. The kids are having lunch right now, and Colleen and Tucker offered to take over for a little bit. It's been a lot more emotional than I thought it would be."

"Really? Some sad stories?"

"Yeah, but the main one is this boy, Dylan. He's the cutest little thing with red hair and freckles and these bright green eyes. He sat down next to me yesterday and told me that his mother had left him when he was a baby and his father died. I spoke to one of the counselors who told me his father committed suicide a few months ago."

"Oh my goodness," Janine said, holding her hand up to her chest.

"He seems connected to me for some reason, so we spent a lot of time together yesterday and even this morning. He's sort of my new right hand man. I took him on the dock and showed him how to bait his hook," he said, smiling slightly.

"He probably looks at you like a father figure. It's got to be hard losing your parents that way."

"Yeah. I just don't know how to help him. I'm not a counselor, and I won't see him again after the next few days. I hate that he's stuck in a foster home where he doesn't feel loved either."

"Say, Dawson... Have you ever thought about..."

"What?"

"Adoption?"

Dawson stared at her, his eyes wide. "No. I surely haven't thought of that. I'm a single guy in his forties. I don't even think they let people like me adopt a kid."

Janine waved her hand at him. "Sure they do! These kids need good homes. You just have to go through the home study process. I bet if you asked a few questions..."

"No. It's a nice idea, but I'm busy running the inn. I'm not married. I have my contracting business..."

"You do realize that parents sometimes work, right? I don't think that precludes you from adopting a child."

Dawson stared off into space. "You know, I always thought I'd be a father one day. Even after I lost my son, I figured it would happen. I'd meet somebody, get married again, have that whole white picket fence lifestyle. I used to imagine those fun Christmas mornings with all of us in matching pajamas, hair all messed up, while we opened presents."

"That sounds nice. What's holding you back from having all of that?"

"I don't know. My life isn't quite what I thought it would be at this stage. Why did I have to meet Julie so late in life? Can you imagine the amazing family we could've built together?"

Janine reached over and squeezed his hand. "It's not too late. Y'all aren't eighty year old people at the nursing home, Dawson. You're both in your forties. And they say forty is the new twenty."

Dawson laughed. "Trust me, forty is not the new twenty. When I get up in the morning, everything has started to crack and now I make this grunting noise when I stand up."

Janine laughed. "You know, if you want to marry my sister, you have my blessing."

He smiled. "Oh, I want to marry your sister. I just don't think she wants to marry me."

"You'll never know if you never ask."

"Do you know something that I don't?" he asked, squinting his eyes at her.

"No, actually I don't. My sister talks in circles just like you do every time I bring up marriage. But the rest of us see that you two are perfect for each other."

"I just think Julie would be happy dating for the rest of our lives, but I'm not sure that's enough for me. The longer we're together, the more I want her there. I hate going to our separate houses at the end of the day. I hate calling her my girlfriend instead of my wife."

"Michael really did a number on her head. And you're nothing like him. She knows that. But I think that's what scares her the most."

"It scares her that I'm not like Michael?"

Janine nodded. "Losing Michael was hard. That was a twenty-one year marriage that fell apart. But, she loves you way more than she ever loved Michael, so losing you might just do her in. I think that's what she's really afraid of. Rocking the boat and messing everything up and never finding that kind of love again."

Dawson nodded his head. "I have the same fear. Do I want to take the chance of getting rejected or do I just want to leave things like they are and be thankful for them?"

Janine chuckled. "Relationships aren't easy, are they?"

~

Meg sat, nervously fidgeting with her hands. Why had the dean called her in to see him? She'd only met him once in passing, and even though it was just a community college, nobody wanted to get called into the dean's office.

"Sorry to have kept you waiting, Miss Pike."

She looked up to see Dean Clayton standing there, his large belly protruding out of his sport jacket. He was the epitome of a college professor complete with elbow patches. He shook her hand and sat down.

"No problem."

"I'm sure you must wonder why I've called you here today?"

"Yes, sir, I was wondering about that." Her hands were now sweating, which they never did. Just great.

"Professor Calvert has recommended you for the teaching assistant program. She said you've done remarkably well in advertising class, so she'd like for you to become her assistant for the fall semester coming up."

"Really?" Meg was shocked. Although she had done well in her advertising class, she never expected that Professor Calvert would want to work with her.

"Would you be interested?"

"Absolutely!" For a moment, she thought about Vivi and how this would affect her schedule, but then she decided that she had to be responsible. Creating a brighter future for herself would only help her daughter, and she'd work out the babysitting issues when and if they came up.

"Excellent. I just have some paperwork here for you to fill out, and then we will be in touch about some training you'll need to do." He slid the paperwork toward her. "I hope you realize what an honor this is. Many students want to be teaching assistants, but don't get the chance. Seize the opportunity, okay?"

Meg smiled. "Oh, trust me. I won't waste this second chance, Dean Clayton."

CHAPTER EIGHT

"Go, go, go!" Dawson yelled as he watched the kids race in potato sacks across his lawn. A couple fell down as soon as he blew the whistle, but Tucker had helped them back up again. Dylan, ever the little competitor, was ahead at first but then one of the older boys took the lead and won the race.

Dawson walked over and squeezed Dylan's shoulder. "Good try, buddy!"

"I hate being short!"

"You won't be short for long. One day, you'll just start growing like a weed, and before you know it you'll probably be taller than me."

Dylan looked up at him. "And then I'll beat everybody in a race," he said, giggling.

"Probably so. I used to win all the races because my legs are so long."

"Kids, time for lunch!" Colleen called. Dylan licked his lips and ran off, eager to have pizza and cupcakes.

"I love those long legs of yours," Julie said, pinching him in the side.

"Oh, hey. When did you get here?"

"A few minutes ago. I got to watch the potato sack race. You see this little bump on my nose?"

Dawson looked closer. "Oh, yeah. I've never noticed that before. It's pretty grotesque."

She smacked him on the arm. "Stop it. Anyway, I got this when I broke my nose doing the three-legged race with Kathy Schulman. She had the worst coordination of any kid I knew. She would literally trip over her own feet. Miss Dial, my fourth grade teacher, made us be partners, and down I went, busting my nose on the hard Georgia clay. Blood everywhere."

Dawson stared at her. "Well, that was a very dark story."

She laughed. "Sorry. I thought it was relevant. How's everything going?"

"Good. Only two more days after today. I'll miss these kids."

Julie wrapped her arms around his waist. "I've been missing you."

"I know. Everything seems so busy these days. How's Vivi?"

"Good. I kept her this morning while Meg met with the dean."

"She met with the dean? Everything okay?"

"Yes. She actually got offered a teaching assistant position for next semester. I'm so proud of her!"

"That's awesome. Please tell her I said congratulations."

Julie looked up at him. "I've been thinking about what you said the other day. You know, about going to our separate homes every night?"

"Yeah?"

"I wish things were different too. I hate being apart so much."

He froze for a moment. Was she saying something? Was she saying she might want to get married? Should he just ask right now, in the middle of kids eating pizza and screaming?

"So we feel the same way?"

She rose up on her tiptoes and kissed him. "I think so. Why don't we work on our schedules so we can spend more time together in the evenings? Maybe we can switch off on whose house we go to?"

Dawson felt very let down. She wasn't talking about marriage. She was talking about schedules.

"Sure. Of course. Listen, I hate to run, but Colleen looks frazzled over there. Dinner tonight?"

"Sounds good. I'll come by around seven?"

"Okay." He kissed her on top of her head and started to walk away.

"Hey, Dawson?"

He turned around. "Yeah?"

"I love you. You know that, right?"

"Of course I do. I love you too."

With that, he walked away, unsure of what to do. Which risk did he want to take? The one where he proposed and got turned down, or the one where he lived a life that wasn't quite what he wanted?

~

SuAnn's brow was beaded with sweat. She never got nervous, but for some reason she was today. The pie competition was coming up in minutes, and she'd been pitted against the twelve-year champion, Henrietta Bankston.

"Well, hello, SuAnn. Good to see you again," Henrietta said as she took the station next to hers. All of the competitors were lining up at their makeshift kitchen areas around the convention hall. Visitors milled about, waiting for the competitors to start cooking.

They had a time limit of ninety minutes, barely enough time to make a homemade crust, bake it and then fill it to cook the last forty-five minutes. She'd have to make sure all of her ingredients were prepared so she could hit the ground running.

"Hi, Hen."

"Henrietta," she mumbled under her breath.

The host of the pie baking competition walked to the microphone. It was go time. He tapped the mic. "Hello? Is this thing on? Good afternoon, everyone!"

The small crowd laughed and clapped.

"Welcome to our eighteenth annual Seagrove Spring Fling Pie Bakeoff. Our contestants have been furiously working to make the best pies any of you have ever tasted. Here's how it's going to work. Each contestant will have ninety minutes from the bell to complete their culinary creation. We will then have our judging panel taste each one, without knowing whose it is, and our new winner will be crowned. That person will win a one hundred dollar gift certificate to Seagrove Spa, a framed certificate and this beautiful hand embroidered apron made by our very own Lila Layton from the Busy Bee Embroidery Shoppe!"

Again, the crowd roared. Funny how excited they got about watching six women bake pies. SuAnn looked over and saw Darcy standing in the wings. She'd asked everyone else to stay away, not needing the extra pressure. But,

Darcy had become her right hand in preparing for the bakeoff, so she didn't mind her being there. Darcy gave her a wink as the bell dinged, and SuAnn went to work.

Within a few minutes, she had her pie shell, infused with chocolate, ready to put in the oven. While it baked for ten minutes, she assembled everything else she needed for her chocolate pecan pie with homemade maple chocolate whipped cream. She'd worked so hard for the last week trying to make it perfect, and now was her time.

At first, she'd planned to make a cherry pie, but when the stupid little lattice pieces weren't perfect, she'd given up the idea. Crestfallen, she'd found the chocolate pecan pie recipe at the bottom of the recipe box. Turned out, it tasted way better to her and Darcy during their taste testing, so she went with it.

"You've got this," Darcy whispered from the sidelines, like a quiet little cheerleader. "Don't let that old bat win this again." SuAnn tried not to laugh.

"Don't get me distracted," SuAnn said, waving her hand at Darcy.

She poured and stirred and whisked and fretted, but it started to come together. Every so often, she would cut her eyes over at Henrietta to see what she was doing, but old Hen had her flour and sugar bags stacked up so SuAnn couldn't see what she was doing. She would occasionally glare in SuAnn's direction too.

"Twenty-two minutes left, ladies," the announcer called.

"Are you good?" Darcy asked.

"I think so. Pie's in the oven, looks to be cooking just fine. I'm going to start making the whipped cream now."

"Don't forget that adjustment we made in the maple syrup flavoring."

SuAnn nodded. "You're right. Thanks for the reminder."

It was like a boxing match where Darcy was her corner coach, reminding her of the best way to knock out old Henny. She loved it. As much as she'd promised Janine that she wouldn't get into trouble and ruin their reputation in Seagrove, she still wanted to win, fair and square.

"Oh no..." she heard Henrietta say under her breath. The woman next to her tried not to make eye contact. Nobody really seemed to like old Hen. Too curious, SuAnn finally looked over at her.

"What's the matter, Hen?"

"Henrietta," she said through gritted teeth.

"Never mind."

After a long pause, Henrietta turned to her, a fake smile on her face. "Sorry, SuAnn," she said in that sickeningly sweet Southern accent. "I'm just stressed to the max over here. You see, it seems I've forgotten my vanilla extract that I desperately need for my whipped topping. My pie just won't have a chance without it." She leaned over and whispered, "It's my secret ingredient."

Suddenly, SuAnn felt frozen in time. For the first time in her life, she had an obvious decision between good and evil. On the one hand, she could refuse to let Hen borrow her vanilla extract and gain an advantage for her own pie. On the other hand, she was trying to grow as a human being, and wouldn't depriving her arch nemesis of borrowing her vanilla be an evil thing to do?

Darcy leaned over to SuAnn's ear. "Did she just ask to borrow something?"

"Yep," SuAnn whispered back.

"You're not going to let her, are you?"

"You don't think I should?"

"Of course not! You'll win for sure if hers doesn't come out right."

SuAnn sucked in a deep breath. "For once in my life, Darcy, I think I'll be the bigger person." She turned and handed the vanilla extract to Hen before going back to her own whipped topping. Hen stood there for a moment, like she was shocked, before turning back to her station.

"I can't believe you did that," Darcy lamented.

"Well, I'd rather win fair and square than let Hen have an excuse for why she didn't win."

Maybe she was actually growing as a person after all.

~

Dawson leaned against the tree, watching the kids play a game of kickball out in his side yard. That was something he thought he would never see, not having any kids of his own. But he had to admit it was fun to hear their laughter and watch them enjoy his property.

"Have you ever seen that much energy in one place in your life?" Amy asked as she walked up next to him.

He chuckled. "I don't think so. But I love it."

"Do you have any kids?"

Dawson shook his head. "No, I don't. Always wanted some, though."

"I have three at home myself. They bring a lot of joy to life, but they are the hardest work I've ever done. Sometimes, I go to my job to get a break," she said, laughing.

"Yeah, I can imagine having three of them is a lot of work. I think I'd be happy with just one. But, I'm a single guy in my forties, so I don't think that's happening anytime soon."

She shrugged her shoulders. "I don't know about that. You know, there's always adoption."

Dawson turned and looked at her, still leaning against the tree. "You mean they'd let somebody like me adopt?"

"Are you some sort of serial killer?"

He laughed. "Not yet. But I guess I just thought that they were more looking for families with a mom and dad. Or even single mothers. I don't hear a whole lot of middle-aged single men adopting."

"Well, it's certainly less common, but we have more and more of that. All sorts of people adopt. Gay couples, single men, single women, families with a mother and a father. It really runs the gamut."

"That's good to hear. I mean, kids just need a happy, healthy home."

"So, what are you thinking?"

"About?"

"Are you open to that idea?"

He smiled slightly. "I don't know. It certainly has me thinking. Getting to know these kids has really opened my mind in several ways."

"How so?"

"Well, take Dylan over there. I've spent a lot of time with that kid this week. Sitting out there on that dock fishing made me feel like I had a son of my own. I was actually imparting some wisdom to him," he said with a chuckle.

"Yeah, I've noticed that you and Dylan really have a bond. He needs that. His father was a pretty major drug addict, and when he took his life a few months ago, he left Dylan here without anyone. He has no family, and he was thrown into the foster system in the blink of an eye. And trust me, the foster system is broken. We have a lot of good foster parents, but we also have a lot of them who aren't so good."

"I've been doing some reading online about that. Maybe I could become a foster parent at some point."

"Or, maybe you could become Dylan's dad."

Dawson looked at her, his mouth dropping open slightly. "What?"

"Pardon me for saying so, Dawson, but you already have a connection with Dylan. He needs a home. A kid his age already has trouble finding adoptive parents, and it seems like you might be a good match for him. I saw him immediately connect with you even on the second day."

"Listen, I love the kid to death. I really do. Anybody would be proud to have him as their son, but I don't know if I'm ready for that. I don't want to mess him up."

"It sounds like you might just have a little anxiety about becoming a father. Give it some thought. I don't want to push you. We never want to do that because we want every home to be a permanent, loving home for a kid. But my gut tells me that you becoming Dylan's dad would be the best thing that happened for both of you."

She patted his arm as she walked away, and Dawson couldn't help but think about what she'd said. The idea had already been planted in his head by Janine the other day, and now here he was faced with the actual opportunity of adopting Dylan. Would Dylan want that? Would Dawson be a good dad to an eight-year-old boy? And how would that affect his relationship with Julie? After all, her kids were grown and she had a grandchild now. How would she feel about him having an eight-year-old son to raise?

Why was it that life always seemed so overly complicated? He remembered something his granny had told him years ago. She said, "Dawson, all the best things in life are the most complicated. That's why they're the best things."

That statement seemed truer than ever right now.

~

Julie walked down the street, opting to walk to Dawson's house instead of drive her car. Tonight, she just needed to clear her mind. Everything Dixie and Janine had talked to her about in the last couple of weeks was making her head swirl. She loved Dawson, and she would never want to lose her relationship with him. But was she ready to get married again? Was she ready to open her heart and her life in that way?

To some extent, having two houses and somewhat separate lives gave her the ability to keep control. But how much control did you really have when you were in love with someone? If she lost him, she would be devastated. Having a piece of paper to say that they were married wouldn't take that devastation away.

The other side of it was she didn't even know if he wanted to get married. It sounded like he did, but maybe he was just looking to live together or to have more time together. She couldn't assume that he wanted to spend the rest of his life with her.

As she walked along, the sandy road below her feet, she could hear the sound of children laughing in the distance at Dawson's house. When she really thought about it, it made her sad that he had never had the opportunity to be a father. He would've been a great dad. She often imagined him with a little girl, looking up at him with those loving eyes, asking to dance with him at some father-daughter dance.

And then sometimes she imagined a little boy, looking up at his dad as he learned to fish out in the beautiful waters of the marsh, the cordgrass swaying in the breeze. There was so much he had missed out on, and she felt bad for that imaginary child who never got the opportunity to have Dawson as their father.

Her whole life might've been different if they had met when they were younger. But if she'd never met and married Michael, she wouldn't have Colleen and Meg and now Vivi. So she couldn't regret any of her past decisions because they led to her life right now.

She was a big believer in fate, and things happening the way they were supposed to. And, for reasons she would never really understand, she wasn't supposed to meet Dawson until her marriage fell apart. Life wasn't always a linear path to success or happiness. And it didn't always make logical sense.

As she approached the house, she saw Dawson sitting on the dock with a little boy by himself. They were casting their fishing lines into the water, laughing occasionally. She watched as Dawson would take the little boy's pole, untangle the line and help him throw it back out again. He sat there, so patient and kind, helping to teach him how to bait the hook.

She crouched behind one of the dunes and listened as Dawson talked to him. It was a side of him she hadn't really seen, other than little glimpses of when he would play with Vivi. But she was a baby, and Julie had never seen his interaction with a little kid before.

"I don't think I'm going to get new parents," the little boy said. Julie's heart suddenly ached with a type of pain she never felt before. What a terrible burden for a little kid to have on his shoulders at such a young age.

"You don't know that, Dylan. God might have other plans for you. You just have to keep up the faith."

A tear formed in Julie's eye. Dawson was such a good man, and it must've been very painful for him to sit there and hear this little boy talk about never having a family again.

She didn't know the boy's situation at all, but any kid in foster care must have felt so left behind. Julie couldn't imagine living without a family.

"Everybody that meets me doesn't want me, though. I try to be good, but they just never come back."

"You're a good kid, and the perfect mom or dad is going to come along and scoop you up very soon."

"Mr. Dawson, do you promise?"

"I promise, Dylan. And I'll even say an extra prayer for you tonight, okay?"

Dylan looked up at Dawson, those big eyes taking in everything he said. "Okay. I believe you then."

Julie slid down and sat on the dune, her arms pulling her knees up toward her chest. She descended into a puddle of quiet tears, hoping no one could see or hear her until she could collect herself. Sometimes, life just wasn't fair.

CHAPTER NINE

SuAnn couldn't believe it. For once, she'd done the right thing, and it had cost her the whole competition. She knew she should've told Henrietta Bankston to kiss her hindquarters when she asked to borrow that vanilla extract.

"I told you not to do it," Darcy said, as they cleaned up the cooking area.

"Stop being a know-it-all. It's not becoming." SuAnn threw the rest of her ingredients into her basket. "Let's get out of here before I smack somebody."

She and Darcy started walking toward the large set of double glass doors leading to the parking lot, but not before Henrietta could make one more jab.

"Better luck next time, ladies," she said with a big fake smile on her face. "Hard to beat a twelve-time champion."

SuAnn rolled her eyes. "Congratulations, Hen. Enjoy that spa day. I recommend anything that will help with wrinkles."

Without missing a beat, she turned and walked out the door with Darcy hot on her heels.

"Gosh, I love you," Darcy said when they got to the car.

"I swear, that woman is infuriating. I helped her win, and she just acted like a horse's ass. Who does that? Obviously, her momma never swatted her legs with a switch."

Darcy giggled. "You're all riled up, aren't you?"

"I feel like drinking an entire bottle of cheap wine and eating every poundcake in the bakery."

"Well, then, let's get to it!" Darcy said, taking the keys from her.

"I wasn't being serious."

"You deserve it. You did a great job, and I tasted those other pies. None of them had a thing on you. That whole thing was rigged."

SuAnn looked at her. "You think so?"

"Absolutely. Her pie tasted like crap. Excuse my language, but it did."

SuAnn wasn't sure if she was just trying to make her feel better or if she really meant it. Either way, the idea of drinking some wine and filling up on sugary carbs had grabbed her attention. She'd have to think about the pie bakeoff conspiracy later.

~

"I'm telling you, it was one of the sweetest things I've ever seen in my life, Dixie. My heart melted and then broke."

Dixie opened the roll of quarters and dumped them into the register. "Dawson has a heart of gold. He wants to help everyone in need."

"True," Julie said as she straightened a new shelf display of gardening books. "But, this was more than that. He's developed a strong bond with that little boy, and I worry how they're both going to feel when camp is over tomorrow."

"You think he's interested in being a foster parent or something?"

"I don't know. Maybe."

"How would you feel about that?"

Julie thought for a moment. "I have no idea. I've never considered something like that, honestly. I raised my girls, but it never occurred to me to take in more kids. I suppose that's selfish."

Dixie chuckled. "No, darlin', that's not selfish. Not everyone is in a position to foster children."

"But, I was, Dixie. I had money. I had a nice home, access to great schools. Michael and I were in good health. We could've done it, but it just never dawned on me. I was living in this little suburban bubble that included mostly vapid women playing bunco and taking tennis lessons."

Dixie stared at her for a moment. "Boy, it's hard to imagine you in that life. You fit in here like a duck on water."

Julie considered that a high compliment. "I can't relate to it anymore either. I guess when you have your life all set up and things are easy, you just keep doing the same thing day after day. I had a housekeeper, Agnes, who I loved. Aside from that, I had a bunch of 'friends' that weren't really friends."

"This life is the only one I've known," Dixie said, shrugging her shoulders.

Julie smiled. "Trust me, this life is a real life. What I was living was just a facade. Fake friends. Fake marriage. Fake happiness."

"And now?"

She sat with that question for a moment and then grinned. "Just a beautiful, real, simple little life. I love it."

"So, what about the whole thing with Dawson?"

"I don't even know what he's considering, if anything. I might just be over-thinking the whole thing."

Dixie pointed to Julie's chest. "I think your heart is telling you something. I've always found it's best to listen."

She knew Dixie was right. She always was. But, Julie didn't know what Dawson wanted. She didn't even know what she wanted. As usual, her life seemed to be taking another strange turn.

~

William had never been more nervous in his life. He sat on his newly refurbished boat and waited for what he hoped would be his first group of charter customers. They had called the day before wanting a trip out to the marsh for a guy's bachelor party. Apparently, this group wasn't into drinking and strippers. They had fishing on their minds, and that was fine with William.

"Pssttt..." he heard from the bushes near the dock. Janine poked her head up, all of that curly hair flopping around in the breeze. He loved her hair, even though it ended up everywhere, like a calling card that she left behind to let people know she'd been there.

"What are you doing over there?" he asked, laughing. She popped up and held out a brown paper bag.

"I brought you a sandwich, some chips and a water for your first trip!" She walked onto the boat and handed it to him.

"You made me a sandwich?" Janine wasn't exactly an expert in the kitchen. She could fold her body into a million yoga poses, and she was one of the kindest people he'd ever met. But food preparation? No.

"Fine. Julie made it for me, but I got the ingredients out of the fridge for her."

William chuckled and kissed her nose. "It's the thought that counts. Thank you for bringing this to me because I did forget to eat this morning. Don't you have class soon?"

"I do. But, I couldn't let this momentous day pass without telling you how incredibly proud I am of you, Will." She leaned against the railing. "You took a leap of faith, and I know how hard that is to do. You're going to be successful with this, but, more importantly, you're going to be happy. And that's all that counts. The rest will fall into place."

He hugged her tightly. "I love you, Janine."

"Even though I can't cook, can barely boil an egg and I had to ask Julie where we kept the bread?"

He chuckled. "Especially because of those things." He looked up and saw his charter group walking down the dock.

"Looks like you're on!" Janine whispered before climbing out of the boat and walking toward the road. She turned around one last time to give him a thumbs up sign and blow him a kiss before disappearing.

"You the charter captain?" one of the men asked. William paused for a moment.

"Yes, sir, I am. Welcome aboard."

~

Dawson sat there, his hands on the picnic table. "So, you're telling me the process for adopting one of these kids wouldn't really be that hard?"

Amy nodded. "Most of these kids don't really have any options. They've been in the foster care system for a long time, and their situations aren't likely to change anytime soon. As you can tell, most of them are older, and we see a lot of people wanting to adopt out of the system but they usually want babies or maybe toddlers."

"What about..."

"Dylan?" Amy asked, smiling slightly.

"Yeah."

"He's been in the system for several months now, as you know. We've tried to reach out to his birth mother, but she hasn't responded and she lost her rights a long time ago. Unfortunately, even Dylan's extended family has a lot of turmoil. Drugs, prison. He's had a very difficult start in his life."

Dawson shook his head and felt his jaw clench. If there was anything that upset him, it was when children were mistreated. Having lost his own child, he couldn't imagine how anyone could mistreat theirs. Of course, he also understood addiction. He had friends with that very problem, and he certainly didn't want Dylan to be put in that situation.

"I'll have to give it some thought. It would be life-changing."

"For both of you," she said with a wink. "Look, I am never interested in pushing anyone to adopt a child. But I've seen you with Dylan this last week, and there's been a change in him. He's smiling more. Much more interactive. Eating again."

"Eating?"

"His foster parents were having a lot of trouble getting him to eat. I think he's just been really sad about losing his father. Even though his dad was a complete screwup, that was all Dylan ever knew. They were having to give him nutritional shakes to keep him from going into starvation."

"Wow. I had no idea. I saw him eat three hotdogs yesterday."

Amy laughed. "Because he's happy here. He likes you. He likes this place. He lived in a single wide trailer on the outskirts of town. This must be like a mansion for him."

"Nothing wrong with living in a trailer."

"Of course not. But there is something wrong with living in one in a drug infested neighborhood and having no heat or air. When we picked him up, he was wearing dirty clothes and had no running water either."

"Oh my goodness. Please don't tell me anymore." Dawson didn't think his heart could take it. And the fact that there were thousands of children out there in the same situation made him feel helpless. He wanted to help them all, but it was impossible. The system was so broken that it was hard to imagine anyone could ever fix it.

"Am I interrupting?" Julie asked as she walked over to the picnic table. Dawson quickly looked at his watch.

"Hey. I didn't expect you until this evening."

"Well, Meg got out of class early so I thought I'd come and see if I could lend a helping hand."

"Hi. I'm Amy." She reached up and shook Julie's hand.

"Nice to meet you."

"Amy is the director of the foster care system. We were just talking about some of the kids and their situations."

"You do good work. I'm not sure I could know about all of these sad stories without it breaking my heart."

Amy nodded. "It breaks my heart every day, but I feel like God called me to do this work so I continue on. The best part of my life is when I see one of these kids get adopted into a good home."

"That must be very rewarding."

"It certainly is. Well, I'd better go and see how the kids are doing on their craft project. Colleen and Tucker should be finishing up soon, and then we will go down to the beach for a little free time."

"I'll be over in a little bit," Dawson said, waving as Amy walked away.

"I can't believe tomorrow is the last day. I'm sure you'll be excited to get a little downtime."

Dawson nodded. "It's been pretty exhausting, for sure. But I've enjoyed every minute of it. I wouldn't trade this experience for anything, honestly."

Julie looked like she wanted to say something. "Listen, can I ask you something?"

"Sure."

"Are you thinking about adopting one of these kids?"

He swallowed hard. "I... don't know."

Her face softened and she reached over, putting her hand on top of his. "Dawson, you would make a fantastic father. You deserve to have that kind of unconditional love from a child in your life. If that's what you want to do, I support you, fully."

He let out a sigh of relief. "Really? You'd be okay with that?"

"Of course. I mean, being a single dad is going to have its challenges."

Single dad. She wasn't saying that she wanted to be Dylan's mother. She was saying that she would continue dating him even if he adopted Dylan.

In that moment a swirl of emotions welled up inside of

Dawson. Was she planning on just dating him forever? Did he want to adopt a child and be a single dad for the rest of his life? No. He wanted Dylan to have everything, including a mother who loved him. A mother who would teach him how to treat women. A mother who would bake him cookies and smile as he gave her a homemade Mother's Day card.

But Julie was already a mother of two grown daughters. It wasn't fair to ask her to start all over and parent somebody else's child that she didn't even know.

Was he going to have to make a choice? He didn't know what to think, so he just kept a fake smile on his face.

"Yeah. I'm sure it will be hard. Listen, I really need to get over there and help corral these kids so we can take them down to the beach. Do you mind?"

"Oh," she said, looking surprised. "I thought maybe I could help out?"

"I'm not really sure what to tell you to do. Maybe check with Colleen?"

There was a tension between them, and he knew that Julie didn't understand it. Maybe she would just think he was tired, and that was okay. He didn't want to have a big emotional conversation right now. He wanted to clear his mind and figure out what to do next, but he couldn't seem to do it. It seemed like he had nothing but questions in his head with no answers.

"Okay. I'll do that. See you later?"

He nodded as she stood up. "Sure."

As he watched her walk away, he wondered how he was ever going to live without her if it came to that. Or should he make the choice to live without Dylan? Could he ever forgive himself now that he knew how much Dylan needed him? Right now, he wanted to walk far out into the ocean until his mind cleared.

~

Julie stood at the table handing out snacks with Colleen before they were going down to the beach for some free time with the kids. So far, she'd met two sisters, ages ten and twelve, who had been in separate foster homes for eighteen months. Another little boy, who was just about to turn seven, had been in the system since he was five years old. The stories were breaking her heart. How had she not seen this before? Had she been so focused on her own bubble of a world that she didn't think about kids without parents?

"You okay?" Colleen asked as she handed out the last bag of baby carrots. The kids walked over to sit at some temporary picnic tables they'd assembled in Dawson's side yard.

"Yeah, I'm fine. These stories are just killing me."

"I know. All week, I've thought about nothing else. I hope that I can become a foster parent one day."

Julie smiled. "Really? That makes me proud of you, my beautiful daughter."

"You know, Dawson and Dylan really have a bond."

She nodded. "I know. I honestly think he's considering adoption," she whispered.

"Really? That would be amazing for both of them."

"It would." Julie wiped down the table and stacked the rest of the snacks into a cooler for next time.

"Mom?"

"What?"

"What's wrong?"

"Nothing's wrong. Why would something be wrong?" Julie said in a voice several octaves higher than her normal one.

"Do you not want Dawson to adopt Dylan?"

She sighed. "I would love that, Colleen. What kind of person wouldn't?"

Colleen put her hands on Julie's shoulders and turned her around. "Then what's going on?"

"It's silly."

"Just spit it out," Colleen said.

"It's just that I feel like he's moving on without me. I mean, he'll become a single dad and be busier than ever, and then maybe we won't be together anymore. How incredibly self-centered is that thought?"

Colleen took her hand and walked her beside the barn where they were out of sight and out of earshot. "Mom, you know that Dawson isn't Dad, right?"

"Of course."

"He would never just leave you like that. If he decides to adopt Dylan, you know it would be after he thought about it long and hard, and he'd want you to be a part of that."

"I'm smart enough to know that Dawson wants the whole white picket fence life. Once he has a son to raise, he's going to want a wife too."

"Why can't that wife be you?"

Julie shrugged her shoulders. "Well, he hasn't asked, has he?"

Colleen's eyes widened. "Come on now, Mom! You know he's hinted and you've shot that idea down before. Why would he ask?"

"I wasn't ready then. Your father... Nevermind. Let's not rehash that."

"Does Dawson know you're ready now?"

"I don't even know if I'm ready now."

Colleen threw her hands up. "Stop overthinking everything! You love him, he loves you."

"Didn't you turn Tucker down?" Julie pointed out, her eyebrows raised.

"Not because I didn't want to marry him. He asked me way too early in our relationship. But, one day, I will say yes if he asks again."

"Sorry to interrupt, but we're heading down to the beach and could really use a couple of extra hands," Tucker said, poking his head around the side of the barn.

"We'll be right there," Colleen said. Tucker trotted away, gathering up a couple of stray kids as he ushered them toward the shoreline. "We'll talk about this later, okay?"

Julie smiled. "Don't worry about me, honey. I'll be fine. You just enjoy the success of this wonderful camp and let me figure out my own relationship problems."

"Fine, but consider one thing."

"What?"

"*You* might just be your only relationship problem, Mom."

As she watched Colleen walk away, she wondered if her daughter was right. Was she the one causing her own issues by living in the past and being afraid of the future?

CHAPTER TEN

Colleen took a long sip of her wine and then set it on the table. "The woman is exhausting."

Dixie laughed. "You better draw those shades so she doesn't see us in here. Besides, I don't need any of my bookstore customers thinking I've turned this place into a bar."

Janine stood up and closed the blinds. She pulled the rolling blind down over the door as well.

"The sun has gone down, so I doubt anybody is even walking around out there. You know why they call us a sleepy little town, don't you?" Janine asked as she sat back down. She poured herself a half a glass of wine, not wanting to miss her early morning class the next day.

"So why did you call this meeting exactly?" Dixie asked. Colleen sighed.

"Is it just me, or are Dawson and my mother two of the most infuriating people you've ever met?"

"What do you mean?" Janine asked.

"The two of them are madly in love with each other, but they have to make everything so difficult. I mean, come on. We know they're going to get married at some point, don't we?"

"That's not necessarily true," Meg said from the corner. She had the baby on her hip and was trying to keep her occupied while the other women sat at the table.

"Do you have some kind of problem with Mom marrying Dawson?"

"Of course not. I like Dawson a lot. But, it's just kind of weird. I mean, she was married to Dad."

"So what? Dad cheated on her, Meg. She doesn't owe anything to him."

"I know that. That's not what I mean. It's just kind of creepy to see her with somebody else."

"Well, you're gonna have to get over that," Janine said, laughing.

"I know. I guess it just bothers me thinking of her going on a honeymoon or something," Meg said, shuddering. Dixie laughed.

"Y'all are cracking me up!"

"So, what happened that made you call us all together?" Janine asked.

"These two need our help. I don't think they're ever going to get it together on their own. On the one hand, you've got Mom thinking that she does want to get married and then she doesn't want to get married and then she worries that Dawson will never ask her. She flip flops like a fish. On the other hand, you've got Dawson thinking about adopting a kid and thinking that Mom would never say yes if he asked her."

"Wait, Dawson wants to adopt a kid?" Meg said.

"I'll tell you about that later," Colleen said, waving her hand at her sister. "The end result is that we have to figure out how to keep these two together. They are our glue."

Janine cocked her head to the side. "Our glue?"

Dixie nodded. "I know exactly what she means. Julie coming to town and getting together with Dawson was what pulled all of us together. Why, if they were to break up, nothing would ever be the same."

"Isn't that a little dramatic?" Janine asked.

"I think Colleen is right. These two are like baby birds who have hurt their wings. We need to pick them up, coddle them a little bit and then send them on their way. Hopefully they fly high." Dixie lifted her arms into the air like she was setting birds free.

Janine stared at her. "And if they don't?"

"Well, that's just not an option," Dixie said, laughing.

"That camp is over tomorrow. I really think Dawson is going to try to adopt Dylan. And if he does, our mother would have to be okay with raising a child all over again."

"Do you think she wants to do that?" Meg asked. "I mean, she's an empty nester. She's a grandmother, for goodness' sake. Would she really want to start all over again?"

"To be fair, she wouldn't really be starting all over. Dylan is eight years old, so it's really just another ten years of her life," Colleen said, thinking out loud. "Still, it's a big responsibility. I don't think she's even spent five minutes with Dylan yet."

"Well, you run that camp. You've got one more day. Why don't you put her with Dylan tomorrow and see if they don't form a bond?" Dixie asked.

Colleen thought for a long moment. "Isn't that a little underhanded?"

"Do you see a problem with that?" Dixie said, shrugging her shoulders.

"Not a problem at all," Colleen said, a slight grin on her

face. “Maybe the only thing we really have to do is make sure that my mom falls in love with Dylan just like Dawson has. Hopefully, that will stoke the fires a little bit to get Dawson to actually propose. Otherwise, this whole thing is going to go on forever.”

“Fine. I’ll go along with this, but we have to accept whatever the outcome is. No pushing of either Dawson or Julie, okay?” Janine said, looking around the room. Everybody nodded.

“Agreed. Tomorrow, we start ‘Operation Fall In Love With Dylan’,” Colleen said with an evil laugh. This just had to work.

~

Julie stood on the end of the dock and stared at Colleen. Even though it was a beautiful day, the salt scented air was blowing her hair away from her face. “Are you serious? I don’t know the first thing about fishing.”

Dylan stood off to the side, his little arms crossed over his chest. “I thought I was fishing with Mr. Dawson today?”

Colleen smiled and looked back and forth at each of them. “Today, we’re trying something new. It’s good to get to know new people, Dylan. So, I thought maybe you could show Miss Julie what you learned from Dawson about fishing.”

“Where’s Dawson?” Julie asked under her breath, her teeth gritted.

“He’s helping set up some games for later. Tucker is working with him.”

Julie looked at Dylan, and he didn’t look amused. After all, what little boy wanted to hang out with a forty-something year old woman he'd only met briefly? Especially when she was dressed in white capri pants and a tank top and looked nothing like a fishing instructor.

"Can Dawson come over here soon?" Dylan pleaded. Colleen ruffled his hair.

"Be good," she said, walking away without looking back. Julie felt like something weird was going on, but she couldn't put her finger on it.

She and Dylan stood there for a moment, each of them looking around like they were on some really awkward date. Finally, deciding that she was the adult, Julie broke the ice.

"So, Dylan, are you going to show me what Dawson taught you about fishing?" She tried to put on her best smile without looking creepy.

"I guess so," he said, dejected. He sat down on the end of the dock, his feet hanging over the edge. His hand rested on the fishing pole that was beside him, and he stared at his knees like they were the most interesting thing in town.

Julie finally sat down beside him, well aware that her white pants would never make it through the day without being stained. She picked up the fishing pole on the other side of her and laid it over one of her legs.

"Look, I know you'd rather have Dawson sitting here. I would if I were you. I don't know the first thing about fishing. But, I'd like to learn if you want to teach me." She didn't really want to learn. But, she needed to do anything she could to salvage this very awkward moment.

He reached for the tacklebox a couple of feet away and popped it open, pulling out a fishing lure. "It's pretty easy. You just put this thing on your hook like this."

She watched him carefully, trying to seem overly interested. Right now, she really just wanted to go back to the bookstore where she felt comfortable. But in the back of her mind, she kept thinking about how Dawson might actually try to adopt this little boy, and he would be in her life. That is, if their relationship survived. Lately, it seemed like Dawson was trying to stay away from her, and that made her feel sad and a little bit nervous.

"Okay. Can you hand me one of those?"

Dylan sighed and reached into the tacklebox, pulling out a bright green worm with glitter inside. It struck Julie that it was kind of cute. She took it from his chubby little hand and attached it to her hook.

"Then you have to turn the little handle like this," he said, obviously not using the technical terms. Julie followed what he did and tightened up her line.

"Like this?"

He nodded. "Then, you flip this little thing over, hold your line and pull your fishing pole back like this," he said, stretching his right arm out beside him. Julie didn't have enough room to do that, so she scooted down a few feet. "And then you swing it out like this and let go of the line. Once it hits the water, you need to reel it in a little bit like this."

Now he seemed to be loosening up. He flung his fishing line out into the water, tightened up the line and then sat there looking at her. She did the same, trying to remember the few times she'd been fishing in her life as a kid.

She pulled her hand back and flung her line, but instead of it going into the water, the hook attached to the back of Dylan's shirt, narrowly missing his skin. Her fishing pole bent, almost to the point of breaking, before she realized what had happened. Dylan, obviously shocked by being caught with the hook, turned his head as far as he could to see what was on his shirt.

Julie stared at him, her fishing pole attached to him. Within seconds, she started laughing hysterically, probably out of nervousness more than anything. "Looks like I caught myself a big one!"

Dylan stared at her, his eyes wide. Thankfully, he started giggling. "I don't think you did that right!"

Before they knew it, they were both crying with laughter as Julie tried to figure out how to get the hook out of his T-shirt. It took a few moments, but she finally did, and she managed to do it without sticking it right through her own fingers.

She laid the fishing pole down on the dock. "Maybe I'm not cut out for this."

Dylan reeled in his line and put it down beside him. "You can't give up. Sometimes things are really hard when you first try them, but you have to just keep trying. If you quit, you'll always be a loser."

She was struck by his matter of fact way of speaking. "Well, I have to say that's very smart, Dylan. And you're right. Quitters never win."

Dylan threw his line back out again while Julie watched him, opting to take a break from her own fishing. For some reason, she felt an urge to get to know this kid. There was no reason to be scared of an eight-year-old.

"So, are you looking forward to going back to school after spring break?"

He shrugged his shoulders as he stared out over the water. "I guess so. I don't really like my school."

"Really? I remember when I was your age, I loved school. They had this thing called Super Kid at my school."

"What is Super Kid?"

"Every week, the teacher could nominate a student to be Super Kid. You got your name on the board in the hallway and this really big pin to wear on your shirt. And then you got to go to the principal's office for a party where you got new pencils and candy."

"We don't have that at my school. Besides, I don't think I'd be nominated for Super Kid."

"Why don't you like school?"

"People make fun of me."

Her heart sank. Julie had never experienced bullying. She'd been lucky to be one of the popular kids for most of her school years. "Why do they make fun of you, Dylan?"

"Because I don't have any parents."

"But you have your foster parents, right?"

He looked at her. "Those aren't real parents. Everybody knows that my mom didn't want me and my daddy died. They call me the poor kid."

"That's wrong. Those aren't very nice people."

"They tell me that nobody really wants me and that my foster parents have me because they get money to keep me. But I think they might be right because I still don't have real parents. Nobody ever picks me."

"Dylan, you're an amazing kid. You're funny and smart and I know the perfect parents are going to come along."

"There are kids in my foster home who are almost teenagers. They told me that they never got picked. What if I never get picked?"

He stared at her with those big green eyes, and she didn't have an answer for him. She didn't understand his life. Thankfully, she had never experienced anything like that. Staring into his eyes, she felt ill equipped to reassure him or answer his questions.

"You can't give up. Remember quitters never win. God has the perfect parents in mind for you."

"But he didn't have the perfect parents for those other kids?"

She wanted to cry. She wanted to run. She felt like the world's worst adult for not having answers for this kid. "You know what, Dylan, life isn't fair. And I would be lying to you if I said I knew the right answer. Sometimes, things just stink. But, I do know that most of the time, things work out in the end."

"I sure hope they work out for me one day. I want a real home with my own room. I'm tired of the kids saying mean things to me."

"I'm sorry, Dylan. I'll say extra prayers for you to find a good home, okay?" Prayers were good, but were they enough for Dylan? Was it a cop out for her to offer to pray but do nothing else to help him?

"Mr. Dawson said the same thing. I hope those prayers work." He reeled in his line again and set his pole beside him. "Sometimes, I miss my dad."

She rubbed his little shoulder. "I'm sure you do. I lost my dad too, and it was very hard."

He nodded. "He did some bad things, but he was my dad. One time, he made me blueberry pancakes and we ate them in bed. That was so fun."

"Blueberry pancakes are my favorite." She didn't know what to say. There was absolutely nothing she could say or do to make it better.

"I wish my dad had been like Mr. Dawson. He's so fun and goofy." Dylan looked at her, a slight smile on his face.

"Yes, he is," she said, smiling herself. "Goofy is a good word to describe him."

"Are you his wife?"

She chuckled. "No, I'm not. We're just really good friends."

"Oh. I think he likes you a lot. He told me how nice you are and that he likes spending time with you."

"He told me the same thing about you," she said. Dylan grinned.

"He did?"

"He sure did. Dawson really thinks a lot of you, and he's pretty smart. Definitely smarter than those mean kids at your school."

Dylan nodded. "I think you're nice."

Julie smiled. "Thank you, Dylan. I think you're very nice too. I'm glad I got to know you today."

"Okay, let's get back to fishing. You can't quit. But this time, please don't catch me instead of a fish!" He giggled and picked up his pole once again. As Julie watched him, she couldn't understand why no one had picked Dylan to be their son, and she couldn't imagine Dawson not becoming his father either.

~

Dixie stood in front of Harry with her hands on her hips. After explaining her plan to him, he still looked confused.

"Are you sure this is a good idea?"

Dixie cackled with laughter. "Honey, I'm never sure anything I think up is a good idea but that hasn't stopped me from doing it."

"What if you cause a whole ruckus?"

She waved her hand at him. "I don't mind causing a ruckus. Sometimes you have to shake things up a little!"

"And you're not going to tell anyone about this?"

She shook her head. "Not a soul. If I tell somebody,

they'll try to talk me out of it, and I know I'm right about this."

"Sugar, it seems a little bit pushy. Don't you think you should let people make decisions for themselves?"

She walked over and sat down beside him on the sofa, squeezing his leg. "People don't always know what's good for them."

"You might ruin a friendship over this."

"I don't think so. Look, I know I'm doing the right thing. Sometimes you just have to take the bull by the horns."

He smiled and leaned over to kiss her on the cheek. "Well, I fell in love with you because you're a spitfire, so I guess I shouldn't try to stop you now."

She laughed. "It wouldn't do you any good anyway, sweetheart. You just be there to back me up, okay?"

"Always."

~

SuAnn stood behind the counter in the bakery, staring out the plate glass window at the square beyond. Today, she was alone because Darcy had to take her baby to the doctor for a check up. She didn't mind being alone as it gave her some time to think.

Traffic in the bakery had been pretty slow today, and she was enjoying the downtime. After the couple of weeks of preparing for the pie bake off, she needed a break. Of course, she would've liked to have won the contest so that all that time was worth it.

Watching Henrietta Bankston win had made her sick to her stomach. That woman didn't deserve anything, and certainly not the title of best pie. She knew hers was better, but she didn't understand the politics of whatever was going on in the town.

"Welcome to Hotcakes," she said as a man walked in. He was well-dressed, wearing a nice suit, and he certainly didn't look like he was interested in eating poundcake. "How can I help you?"

"I'm looking for SuAnn."

"That's me. And you are?"

"My name is Alton Fisher. I'm on the board of commissioners."

"Oh. Nice to meet you," she said, unsure of why he was there.

"I'm going to cut right to the chase. I understand that you competed in the pie bake off a few days ago?" He asked, looking behind him as if he was afraid he was being watched.

"Yes, I did. I was the runner-up."

"Actually, you weren't."

"Excuse me?"

"Look, I don't normally make it a habit to go outside of the ranks of the county commission, but I just couldn't hold my tongue. You see, we found out that there were some inconsistencies in the voting. In a nutshell, you won by several votes. But, Henrietta has a lot more power, if you get my drift."

SuAnn couldn't believe what she was hearing. She stood there, her mouth hanging open. "So, I won?"

"You won."

SuAnn laughed. "So that old bat messed with the votes?"

He struggled not to laugh. "It appears that Henrietta Bankston was involved in some fraudulent behavior, yes.

But I won't go as far as calling her an old bat. Even though I might think so."

SuAnn came out from behind the counter and rubbed her hands down the front of her apron to get the flour off. "Now what?"

"Well, I only found out this information an hour or so ago. You know, I have small kids, and I teach them about integrity and honesty. I just couldn't go without telling you the truth."

"But, is this going to be addressed in some way?"

"I don't know how much you know about small-town politics, ma'am, but it can be worse than what you see in Washington D.C.. I'm not sure I can do anything to help you right the wrong."

"Oh."

"I was hoping just knowing that you were the actual winner would be enough."

"Yeah, it's not. Henrietta Bankston needs to be put in her place."

"I wish I could help you do that."

"Me too."

"Well, I should be going. I hope you'll keep my name out of this?"

She smiled and reached out her hand to shake his. "I will. And thank you for coming here to let me know the real truth. I do appreciate that."

Mr. Fisher turned around and walked to the door, turning back before he exited. "Welcome to Seagrove."

As he walked down the sidewalk, SuAnn smiled to herself. Oh, she was going to get old Hen back if it was the last thing she did.

CHAPTER ELEVEN

Dawson couldn't believe it was the last day of camp. Julie had been there all day helping out, although their paths hadn't crossed very much. He didn't know what to say to her. On the one hand, he wanted to drop to one knee and propose, tell her he was going to adopt Dylan and ride off into the sunset as a happy family.

On the other hand, his stomach churned every time he thought about talking to her about adoption. He didn't want to lose her or their relationship. He loved her more than he could describe, and the thought of things breaking apart were almost too much to bear.

As he watched Dylan play with the other kids, he couldn't imagine not seeing him every day. The last week had been life-changing for him, and he already thought of Dylan like he was his son. Sometimes, he felt like his son, Gavin, was speaking to him from heaven.

In fact, last night he'd had a dream about Gavin. They were out in an old fishing boat, and Gavin was telling him it was time. Dawson kept asking him time for what, but Gavin just kept saying it was time. It startled him so much that he had woken up with his heart pounding.

"Can you believe it's over?" Colleen asked as she walked up beside him.

"I can't. What an amazing week."

"Yeah, I hope we can do this again next year. I've really enjoyed getting to know these kids."

"Me too. It's going to be awfully quiet around here tomorrow."

Colleen walked off to help one of the children tie their shoe, and Dawson looked at Dylan again. He was waving from across the yard, a big grin on his face.

"Hey," Julie said from behind him.

"Hey. I was just telling Colleen how quiet it's going to be here tomorrow."

She walked over and slid her arm around his waist, resting her head just below his shoulder.

"I know you're going to miss these kids, but especially Dylan."

He looked down at her. "Yeah. I like that kid."

"He likes you too. He told me so when we were fishing today."

Dawson laughed. "You went fishing with Dylan?"

"Colleen put us together. I think she thought it was funny, but I ended up putting a hook in the back of his T-shirt."

Dawson laughed loudly. "Really? I would've loved to have seen that!"

"It was a funny moment, but thankfully I didn't hurt him or me. We didn't catch one fish, but we had a wonderful conversation. He's a special little guy. I hope he finds a good home soon."

"Yeah. Me too," Dawson said. It was obvious that she

wasn't thinking that home could be Dawson's. She was thinking of some other family that would come along and sweep him up, and the thought of that made Dawson sad. He wanted Dylan to have a good home, of course, but he wanted it to be his.

"Listen, I want to talk to you later. Do you think we could meet up for dinner down on the dock?"

"Sure. Besides, I have to get going. I need to help Dixie at the bookstore for a few hours."

He nodded. "I'll see you around seven?"

"Seven it is." She rose up on her tiptoes and gave him a quick kiss on the lips.

As she walked off to her car, Dawson wondered what was going to happen after they talked. He didn't even know what he was planning to say. He just knew they needed to clear the air, and he hoped at the end of it they would still be together.

~

Julie walked into the bookstore, her heart heavy. She had a sinking feeling about her meeting with Dawson tonight. Maybe he was going to break up with her. Maybe he would choose to be a single father and focus on that without the added stress of having a girlfriend.

Dixie was on her cell phone behind one of the bookcases when she walked in, so she reached around and stopped the bell from dinging and interrupting her conversation.

"Right... on Sunday... three tiers... green... really beachy..." Dixie turned and noticed Julie standing there. "I need to go, Stella. I'll give you a call back in the morning, okay?" She pressed end on her phone and smiled. "I didn't hear you come in."

Julie sat down in the chair. "I didn't want to interrupt your phone call. What was that about?"

"Well, I wanted to help out with the reception," Dixie said, scrunching her nose.

"What? No! This is our gift to you!"

"I ran into Stella who runs the City Street Bakery. When she told me all that you'd ordered, I just didn't feel right letting you do all of that."

"But she's across town! We thought for sure you wouldn't know her."

"Stella's grandma and I played cards together years ago."

"Of course," Julie said, rolling her eyes. "So that's who you were on the phone with just now?"

"Yes. I was just ordering a little cake so I could smash it in my beloved's face."

"We were getting cake, Dixie," Julie groaned.

Dixie shrugged her shoulders. "You can never have too much cake, darlin'. Don't fret."

"Stella shouldn't have even taken your order. She knows what we've got planned."

Dixie chuckled. "I'm a pushy broad when I want to be. Don't be mad at her. Say, you seem like your feathers are ruffled about something. What's going on?"

Julie put her head on the table. "I think Dawson might be breaking up with me tonight."

"What?"

"He wants to have dinner on the dock at seven to 'talk'."

"And?"

Julie looked up. "When has talking ever been a good thing?"

"You had me worried for a minute. Maybe he just wants to catch up after a busy week."

"Dixie, come on. He specifically wants to talk. That can't be good."

"He loves you."

"And I love him. But, things have been different this week. I think he's planning to adopt Dylan."

Dixie smiled broadly. "That makes my heart feel so warm. Dawson would be a wonderful father to that boy. You don't want him to do that?"

"Of course I do. I just don't know where I fit into that scenario."

"What do you mean?"

"I mothered two daughters. I don't know the first thing about boys. And what if Dawson wants to do this alone? Are we just going to date forever?"

"Wait. Do you want to marry Dawson?"

Julie allowed a smile to creep across her face. "Maybe."

"Oh, doll, I'm so happy to hear that! You know that boy is scared as a cat in a room full of rocking chairs to ask you to marry him."

"You think so?"

"Listen, I know him like the back of my hand, and Dawson wants to propose. I just know it. But, I think he's scared you'll say no."

"I would never say no to Dawson." Hearing the words come out of her mouth were shocking, even to her. Somewhere along the way, she'd gone from never wanting to get married again to desperately wanting to be Dawson's wife.

Dixie grinned and clapped her hands in delight. "What if..."

"What if what?"

"What if *you* proposed to *him*?"

"Are you serious?"

"Come on! Women can do anything these days, right? He won't be expecting that at all! And it will show him how serious you are about building a life with him, even if he adopts Dylan."

"I wouldn't know what to say..."

Dixie pointed at the center of her chest. "Speak from here, darlin'. That's all it takes."

Julie stood up. "I'm going to do it!"

Dixie stood up to join her. "This is so exciting!"

"I feel like I'm going to throw up."

Dixie reached out and put her hands on Julie's shoulders. "You can do this. He loves you. Just remember that."

Julie grabbed her purse and turned toward the door. "Wish me luck!"

~

SuAnn looked across the square and saw Henrietta standing with a group of her friends. She was holding court, like she was some sort of royalty when in fact she was just a cheater.

As she locked up the bakery door, she thought about the best way to approach this. All day long, she had been boiling inside. The thought of how hard she and Darcy had worked on that contest only to have it taken from them by someone who thought she was better than everybody else.

Before she knew it, she felt her feet walking straight in the direction of Henrietta. There she stood, in all her glory with her too tight skirt and her big bouffant hairdo.

She wanted to flick something into her hair and watch it go up in flames. Okay, maybe that was a bit too much. With the amount of hairspray she used that would most certainly cause a flammable event to happen.

"Well, hello, Hen," SuAnn said, her arms crossed. Henrietta and all of her friends, all as equally tacky as she was, turned around. They looked at her with such disdain that it was obvious Henrietta had filled them in on who she was.

"Again, dear, it's Henrietta. What can I help you with?"

SuAnn chuckled under her breath like some sort of maniac. "Well, I was just wondering if you had filled your friends in on what you did at the pie contest?"

Henrietta cleared her throat. "I'm not sure I understand?"

"I think you do. Would you like for me to explain?"

Feeling cornered, Henrietta turned and looked at her friends. "Would you ladies mind giving us a moment alone? Being the mayor's wife is an exhausting job," she said, waving her hand in the air.

"Oh, this has nothing to do with you being the mayor's wife..." SuAnn interjected as her friends, or maybe groupies would've been a better word, walked away. Each of them turned around several times to sneer at SuAnn, looks she returned right back to them.

Henrietta turned around quickly and stared at her, her eyes squinting. "What in the world is this about?"

"Well, your tone certainly changed quickly."

"I don't know what you're getting at about the pie contest. I won fair and square, and it sounds like you've got a lot of sour grapes!"

"I know you cheated."

Henrietta rolled her eyes and scoffed. "Oh good Lord,

this is unbecoming. Losers should lose with dignity. Second place is still good. But don't lower yourself by making false accusations."

SuAnn smiled. "I know that you cheated. A little birdie told me, and if you'd like I can certainly get the proof to show at the next county commission meeting."

The color drained out of Henrietta's face. She stood there, her arms by her side, no expression whatsoever. "No one will believe you."

"Oh, I think they will. Didn't your momma ever tell you that cheaters never prosper."

"What do you want from me?"

"I want you to set the record straight. I won that contest, and we both know it."

Henrietta walked over and sat down on a metal bench. She looked as dejected as anyone SuAnn had ever seen. "I don't know what got into me. I won that contest for twelve years in a row. When I found out that you were about to break my streak, something just sent me right over the edge."

SuAnn couldn't believe her ears. Was this woman actually admitting what she'd done? That seemed very out of character for her.

"I'm new here. That contest was important for me and for my business."

"I understand that. I truly do. You know, times are really changing around here. When my husband first took office years ago, we were a big deal. Everybody looked up to us. I went to all of the best parties, and we were always invited to everything. But now all of this new blood is winning the elections, and it's only a matter of time before we're booted out of office."

"What does that have to do with a pie competition?"

"It was all I had. It was my claim to fame, even though that's ridiculous. Hearing myself say it out loud makes me feel like a loser."

"You shouldn't define yourself by these kinds of things, Hen."

"Henrietta."

SuAnn waved her hand. "See? Henrietta sounds pretentious. Why can't you just let me call you Hen?"

"Because a hen is an animal, not a person. It's not proper."

"Don't you ever get tired of keeping up appearances?"

"I suppose so. Sometimes. But I'm far too old to change who I am now. Look, I'm sorry for what I did. I don't really know how to make it better. I guess I can go admit what I did, and then you can have the crown and the spa certificate..."

"I don't want the prizes. I just wanted to know I accomplished something here in my new home. It's lonely sometimes, even though my family is here. They're all busy," SuAnn said, sitting down next to her.

"I know what you mean. My son moved all the way to Atlanta in search of some fancy job. My daughter got married and moved out to some godforsaken ranch in Montana. I never see my grandchildren because they live too far away. And my husband, well let's just say he's not the most entertaining fellow I've ever met."

SuAnn laughed. "I just got divorced because I got addicted to shopping on those TV stations and ended up spending a ton of money. And my husband was as boring a man as I've ever met. I had to do something to entertain myself."

The two women looked at each other and started laughing. "Why, aren't we a pair?" Henrietta said.

"Yeah, I guess we are more alike than I thought we were."

"Say, do you think we might be able to become friends?"

SuAnn thought for a moment. "I guess anything is possible. But first, you have to make things right."

"I will," Henrietta said. "I promise."

~

Dawson stepped aboard William's boat, the water causing him to bob up and down as other boats made their way home for the day.

"How's business so far?"

William laughed. "Well, I've been in business less than a week, so I'm not a millionaire just yet. But, things are going well."

"Good. Congratulations, man." Dawson sat down and leaned his head back, running his fingers through his hair.

"What's up?"

"What do you mean?"

William sat down across from him. "Dude, I've known you since we were kids. You're always stressed when you lean back and run your fingers through your hair."

Dawson sat up and looked at him. "You mean I have a tell?"

"Let's just say you wouldn't be good at poker."

"I've got a lot on my mind, and I just had to get away from the inn for awhile. Camp ended this afternoon, and things were so quiet after those kids left."

"Yeah? I bet you'll enjoy that quiet," William said with a laugh.

Dawson scrunched his face. "Is it crazy if I said I don't

enjoy it? That I miss those kids? Or, specifically, one of those kids."

"Janine told me you've formed a bond with one. Dylan, I think?"

Dawson smiled. "He's a cool kid. The situation he was in... Man, I can hardly think about it without my eyes tearing up."

"Bad stuff, huh?"

"Yeah. But..."

"But what?"

"I'm thinking about adopting him, if they'll let me."

William stopped what he was doing and looked at Dawson. "Seriously?"

"Do you think that's a crazy idea?"

"I think it's really noble."

"Nah, it's not noble. It's just that I love that kid. I don't want to save him. I kind of feel like he'd be saving me."

"How so?"

"I've wanted to be a dad for as long as I can remember. You know that."

"What about Julie?"

"Well, see, that's the thing. I don't know how she'd feel about being married to me and raising a son."

"Married? Have y'all even talked about that?"

Dawson shook his head. "Not really. At least, not in a few months. Getting her to marry me is going to be hard enough after everything Michael put her through, but asking her to start over and be the parent of an eight year old might put the last nail in the coffin."

William leaned forward, his elbows on his knees. "I think you're wrong about Julie. I see how she looks at you, man. She's a good woman, and there's no way she'd leave you because you want to adopt Dylan."

"I don't even know if I'd qualify to adopt him. There's so much red tape involved. But, I'd at least like to try, you know?"

"Is there a reason why you don't just propose to Julie?"

"Are you insane? I can't just propose without even talking about marriage beforehand. She's not a spur of the moment kind of person. She's more of a planner."

"She literally moved here on the spur of the moment and started a whole new life. What makes you think a surprise proposal wouldn't be the most romantic thing that's ever happened to her?"

Dawson sat with the idea for a moment while William finished getting his stuff together to go home for the day. What would happen if he just went straight to the jeweler before they closed, picked the perfect ring and popped the question by the ocean in a few hours?

"What if she says no?"

William slapped him on the back. "Then you'll have your answer. What good is it to keep dating if you want to be a married man? And, at least you'll know where you stand, right?"

"Right." Dawson said as he climbed out of the boat. "I just hope I'm not standing alone."

CHAPTER TWELVE

Julie sat in her car, her hands shaking as they gripped the steering wheel. What had she been thinking? She was going to pop the question to Dawson? Had she gone insane? Dixie could talk her into anything. Well, at least nothing had happened yet. He had no idea she was thinking such a crazy thought, and he never would. At least no harm was done.

She could see him off in the distance, casting his fishing line out into the water as he waited for her to get there. Why was she so nervous? He wanted to talk to her, and that never seemed like a good thing. In her experience, when a man - or anyone, really - said they wanted to talk, it wasn't because they wanted to chat about how great things were going.

After finally summoning her courage, she stepped out of her car and started walking toward him. He was so handsome, standing there in his khaki shorts, baby blue t-shirt and boat shoes. Tall and strapping, as her mother would call him, he was the epitome of movie star handsome. The way he moved, so lithe and strong, made her feel safe when he was around. He was the whole package of strong and sexy and kind that every woman wanted, and she got to call him her boyfriend. What would it be like to call him her husband?

That was it. She was going to do this. She was going to propose. She was going to go for it! She marched toward him like she was on a military mission, and she wasn't going to lose. This was her moment, and she was grabbing that brass ring. Going for that gold medal...

"Peach cobbler?" Suddenly, Lucy appeared out of nowhere in front of her. She was holding a dish wrapped in aluminum foil, a big smile on her face.

"What?"

"Peach cobbler. You love it, right? I made it for your dinner with Dawson. You take it to him?"

Julie laughed under her breath, her adrenaline still pumping like she'd been chasing a lion. "Of course. Thank you, Lucy. Good to see you."

As Lucy made her way back into the house, Julie tried to catch her breath. All of that courage and bravery she'd just mustered had escaped and she was left with a pounding heart and boatloads of stress hormones coursing through her veins. As much as she loved Lucy, she wanted to pinch her hard right about now.

"Oh, you're here," Dawson said, a broad smile on his face. Why was he so good looking? It made it very hard to concentrate sometimes, especially when the setting sun was casting orange and yellow light on his stubbled jawline.

"Lucy gave me this," she said, handing it to him. He set it on the picnic table behind him and then pulled her into a tight embrace. Okay, this was a good sign. He wouldn't hug her like that if he was dumping her, right? Or maybe it was a long goodbye hug to last her the rest of her life?

~

As Dawson held her in his arms, he didn't want to let go. What if she said no to his proposal? What if she laughed? What if she said he had to choose between her and Dylan?

Finally, he pulled back and looked down at her. She was so beautiful, especially in the streaking lights of a lowcountry sunset. "Ready to eat?"

"Sure," she said, seeming a little nervous. Maybe she was trying to figure out how to let him down easy, tell him if he adopted a kid she was moving on with her life.

"Lucy made brisket today, so I hope that's okay?"

"I love her brisket. And her baked beans. That woman is a whiz in the kitchen, huh?"

Was her voice shaking? Something was different, but he couldn't put his finger on it.

"I hear y'all are planning a surprise wedding reception for Dixie and Harry this Sunday?"

She stared at him. "Please tell me Janine asked if we can have it here?"

He laughed. "She did. Lucy is all prepared to help out. Of course, I'll do whatever y'all need me to do."

"We'll need the arbor pulled down to the beach. I thought it'd be a nice touch to have them renew their vows in front of the water with Reverend Lumpkin."

"That sounds great," Dawson said, unable to take in her words as he tried to formulate what he wanted to say. He passed the bowl of baked beans to her.

"So, you said you wanted to talk to me about something?"

Crud. He wasn't ready yet. He needed more time to not sound like a moron when he asked her. He had to stall.

"Well, I wanted to talk to you more about Dylan."

"Dawson, I already told you that I think you adopting him would be a great idea."

"I know. But, I guess I'm wondering where that would leave us?"

There was a long pause. Longer than he liked or anticipated. "I love you. That's all that matters, right?"

Not what he wanted to hear. That was a non-answer. Maybe he should just abort this mission and be okay with single dad-hood and long-term dating.

No. It was time to go for broke. Put it all out there. Lay it on the line...

"Julie, I..."

"You forgot the sweet tea!" Lucy suddenly called out from the side door. Dawson felt like he might have a heart attack.

~

That darn Lucy! She had the world's worst timing. Just when Julie thought she was brave enough to say the words... to ask *the* question... Lucy had yelled out the door and scared them both to death.

Dawson put the tea on the table and let out a breath. "She scared me."

"Me too."

"Listen, do you want to take a walk on the beach before the sun finishes setting? The food is hot, so we can come right back."

"Sure. I'm not sure I can eat right now anyway. She startled me," Julie said, laughing. The truth was, her stomach was churning like a million butterflies were in there having a keg party.

He took her hand and led her onto the fluffy sand. As they got closer to the water, it was more packed and easier to walk. She could smell that salty sea air, and it started to calm her in the way it always did. Being with Dawson by the ocean was her favorite place to be.

"I visited with William today. Sounds like his fishing charter business is going really well," Dawson said.

"Yeah, Janine said he's really happy. I'm always happy for people when they find happiness." What kind of a stupid sentence was that? How many times had she just said happy?

They walked a bit without speaking, and Julie tried to summon the courage to just ask the question. Finally, they stopped, the sun starting to disappear behind the horizon. Dawson turned around and held both of her hands.

"I need to talk to you about something else."

She took a deep breath and blew it out. "I know. But before you do that..."

"I just can't keep going on like this..." he said at the same time.

"But I just need to say..."

"If you'll just let me speak for a minute..." he said.

"Will you marry me?"

"Will you marry me?"

Wait. What had just happened? Had they both just asked each other to get married at the same time? They stood there for a moment, staring at each other, both of their mouths hanging open. It was like time was standing still and they were both frozen. She wondered if she was still alive.

"Did that just really happen?" she asked, her heart pounding in her chest.

"I think so. Did you just propose to me?"

"I did. Did you just propose to me?" she asked, smiling.

He laughed. "I did."

"Oh my gosh. We just proposed to each other at the same time?"

"That seems to be the case. I never expected *you* to propose to *me*."

"And I was afraid you would never ask me, so I decided to take the bull by the horns at Dixie's urging."

"Yeah, I kind of got the same speech from William today."

Again, they just stood there staring at each other for a moment. "So does that mean you felt pressured to ask me?"

He ran his thumb down her cheek. "Absolutely not. I've been wanting to ask you almost since the moment we met. But I knew you weren't ready after the whole fiasco with he who shall not be named."

"Yes, let's not name him."

"Did you feel pressured by Dixie?"

"No. She encouraged me to do what I already wanted to do. I have known for months that I wanted you to be my husband one day."

"I have to ask. What about Dylan?"

"What about him?"

"I mean, if we get married and I adopt him, you would be his mother."

"You can't adopt him, Dawson."

He looked at her, his face falling. "What? So if we get married, Dylan can't be..."

She put her hand on his chest. "Relax. I just meant that

you can't adopt him alone. I think we should do it together if we're both going to be his parents."

He grabbed her in the tightest hug she'd ever felt in her life, his face pressed down into her shoulder. She didn't know, but she swore that she felt him choking up.

"Are you serious? We're going to get married and adopt a kid?" She'd never seen his face look that excited.

"Well, I don't know because you haven't answered my proposal yet."

He smiled. "You haven't answered *my* proposal yet."

"Dawson Lancaster, the most handsome man I've ever met in my entire life, will you do me the honor of becoming my husband?"

"Absolutely, I will." He leaned down and kissed her before dropping to one knee. He reached into his pocket and pulled out a small blue box and opened it, revealing a simple diamond engagement ring with a round stone. "And Julie Pike, will you do me the honor of becoming Julie Lancaster, my beautiful wife and mother of Dylan?"

She nodded her head, and grinning from ear to ear. "Yes!"

He picked her up and swung her around in circles until she felt like she might get vertigo. When he put her down, she held onto his arms to stabilize herself.

"Now what?"

He chuckled. "I don't know, you're the woman. What kind of wedding do you want? I would marry you right here, right now."

Julie started laughing. "I don't want a big wedding. I just want to say our vows in front of our family and friends at some kind of small get together. Does that work for you?"

He let out a long sigh of relief. "Yes. I don't want to

wait and plan a big wedding. I want to say our vows and be husband and wife as soon as possible."

"I can't believe this is happening." Her cheeks were starting to hurt from smiling so much.

"Neither can I. We're going to be a family, Julie. A real family."

Her eyes widened. "I am going to be the mother of a boy. I don't know what that's going to be like."

He cupped her cheeks in his hands and lightly kissed her on the nose. "You're going to be the best boy mom. I love you."

"I love you too. Now, can we go eat that brisket because I'm starving!"

~

Julie busied herself with getting the reception set up. It was all she could do to concentrate on what she needed to do for Dixie and Harry because she was so excited about her own engagement.

So far, she and Dawson had managed to keep it under wraps. They didn't want anyone to know they were engaged just yet so as not to take the limelight off of Dixie's big day.

Friends and family were there and William had gone to get his mother. Although Dixie already knew about the party, nobody else knew that except her closest friends. They wanted the other guests to treat it like a surprise party.

She and Dawson had stayed up most of the night of their engagement, laughing and talking and planning. He had even taken the time to email Amy with their intent to adopt Dylan. She really felt that the process would go smoothly, especially if both of them were going to be adopting him. She recommended waiting until after they got married to file the paperwork so as not to throw anything off. That just made Julie and Dawson want to get married more quickly.

"Hello, my fiancée," Dawson said, pressing his lips to her ear. It sent shivers up her spine every time he did that.

"You better be quiet if you want to keep this a secret." She wiggled away from him and put the big bowl of fruit on the buffet table.

"I can hardly keep it to myself. Everybody is going to be so shocked and excited," he said.

"Who's going to be shocked and excited?" Janine asked as she walked up.

"Dixie, of course. She has no idea what a great party we've planned here," Julie said. Dawson gave her a sideways glance, and she struggled not to laugh.

"William texted me a few minutes ago and said that they are only about five minutes away so we should probably hide soon."

"Right. You go tell that side of the lawn and I'll tell this side."

They went around getting everybody to hide on the other side of the house so that when Dixie walked up the walkway with her new husband, everybody would jump out. She hoped they didn't give her a heart attack or something.

As they hid beside the house, Dawson wrapped his arms around her from behind. They had barely been separated since saying yes to each of their own proposals. It was just proof that they had the most unique relationship that both of them had ended up proposing in the same moment.

"Where do you want to go on a honeymoon?" he whispered in her ear.

"Hawaii? Paris? Cancun?"

"I will go anywhere you want to go."

She looked up at him and whispered. "Honestly, we could stay right here on this beach and I would be happy as a clam." Dawson smiled.

"There she is," he said as a car pulled up. William got out and walked around to help his mom out of her door. Harry was in the back and followed as they went up the walkway.

Julie held up her fingers and counted down three, two, one...

"Surprise!" everybody yelled. Dixie, ever the showman, put her hand over her heart as if she was shocked to her core. It was funny when Julie thought about it.

"Oh my goodness! What is this? It's not my birthday."

"We wanted to celebrate your wedding by throwing you a surprise reception!" Julie said, calling on all of her non-existent acting capabilities.

Dixie played along and spent the next thirty minutes walking around and chatting with everyone. The party was fun and lighthearted, a DJ playing big band music in the background.

As everyone mingled, all Julie could think about was when and where she and Dawson could get married. She looked out at the beach where the arbor was set up, the beautiful purple flowers draped over it, and thought how perfect it would be to just walk out there right now and say I do.

"It's beautiful," Dixie said as she hugged Julie. Dawson walked away for a moment to chat with some of the other guests.

"I'm glad you like it, and also you should be an actress," Julie said under her breath.

"I'm so thankful for this wonderful party. Did you see the beautiful wedding cake that Stella made?"

"I did. Although I'm not sure why you ordered such a large cake for this? It's beautiful with the green and the sea shells. Exactly what I would've picked."

Dixie smiled. "Oh, I don't know. I just thought we might need it."

Julie didn't know what that meant. Maybe she was planning on taking a lot of it home for leftovers, although she was doubtful Dixie would be able to consume quite that much sugar.

"Everyone, if I can have your attention, Reverend Lumpkin is here so that the newlyweds can reenact their vows for us down on the beach. If everyone can start heading that way," Julie called to the crowd.

Everyone walked down and took a seat in the white folding chairs that had been set up for the occasion. Dixie and Harry, dressed in their Sunday best, walked down to Reverend Lumpkin. He said a few words, and then they faced each other, holding hands and smiling.

"Harry, I love you."

"Dixie, I love you too."

Julie looked at Dawson. "Those were their vows? I hope ours are a little bit more in depth than that."

Dawson chuckled. "Yeah, that was kind of weird."

Without warning, Dixie turned to the crowd. "Okay, folks, I have something I need to say. We appreciate this party more than you will ever know. My new husband and I have been married for months, and we didn't need a big shindig like this. But I have the best friends and family in the world, and I'm so thankful for what you've done here today. However, I have to admit that I might have figured out what was going on ahead of time."

Now Julie really was confused. Why was Dixie letting the cat out of the bag?

"I hate to ruin the surprise, but I have to because I actually have a different surprise in mind for today."

"Dixie, what are you doing?" Julie whispered loudly.

"Well, you see, there are two people here at this party who need this altar and this Reverend more than we do. I'm talking about two people who are the glue of our group. Two people who adore each other and deserve a lifetime of happiness. So, Harry and I would like to give up this reception and this beautiful flower covered arbor to those two people if they would like to use it to get married right now."

A hush fell over the crowd except for the occasional gasp and quiet murmuring. Julie looked around, as did Dawson. Then, they realized everyone was looking at them.

"What's going on?" Dawson stammered.

"I think you know what's going on," Dixie said, winking at him. She and Harry walked over to Julie and Dawson.

"How did you know we were engaged?" Julie asked.

"Oh, I didn't. I just had a feeling that you two needed a little push, so I set this up. I bought you a cake, and the wedding march is ready to be played. Oh, and I have these rings." She held up two simple gold wedding bands.

"We got engaged last night," Julie said. "You don't have to give up your reception for us. We're going to get married anyway."

"Then why wait?" Dixie asked, a big smile on her face.

"You're crazy. But we love you."

"Then let's see some I do's," Dixie said, pointing at the altar.

"Do you want to?" Dawson asked.

"I do. Do you want to?" Julie asked, grinning.

"Absolutely!"

They walked over to the altar and stood in front of each other. It wasn't what Julie had ever imagined. She was standing there in a long floral maxi dress, and Dawson was wearing khaki pants and a polo shirt, but somehow it was perfect.

"Dearly beloved, we are gathered here to celebrate the marriage of Dawson and Julie..."

Julie didn't hear much of what the Reverend said as she stared up into Dawson's eyes. She'd never imagined her day would end like this, getting married to the man of her dreams. She scanned the crowd and found her mother and daughters sitting together. All of them were grinning, and SuAnn even gave her a thumbs up.

"Do the bride and groom have vows they would like to recite?"

"Well, seeing as how this was a total surprise, I don't have anything prepared but I'm willing to wing it," Julie said, laughing. The crowd laughed right along with her.

"Very well then," the Reverend said.

"Dawson, you came into my life at a time when I didn't know who I could trust. You were this wild card I didn't expect. I didn't even expect to live here, in this place I'd never heard of. And somehow, you were exactly what I needed. I now know that everything I've gone through in my life has led me here to you, and I couldn't be happier to be Mrs. Julie Lancaster."

Dawson teared up and squeezed her hand.

"Julie, you were also the most unexpected gift. After

the grief I've experienced in my life, I never expected to fall in love again, and certainly not with a woman who had only accidentally shown up on my doorstep. From the moment I met you, I knew that you were special. Thank you for agreeing to marry me, and I promise I will always protect you and do everything I can to make you happy."

As the minister had them exchange rings, Julie couldn't believe it was happening. Her life was coming full circle, and there was nothing she could have ever imagined that would've been more perfect than this moment.

"I now pronounce you husband and wife. Dawson, you may kiss your bride!"

He grabbed her tightly, pressed his lips to hers and dipped her sideways until she was almost touching the ground. When they finally came up for air, he raised her hand into the air with his.

"We got hitched!" he yelled into the crowd as everybody laughed and clapped. She was Mrs. Lancaster, and everything was great in the world.

EPILOGUE

Julie reached into the refrigerator and pulled out the chilled watermelon. Setting it carefully on the counter, she retrieved a large knife from the drawer and handed it to Dawson.

"Have fun," she said as he started cutting. She couldn't believe that it was already Sunday dinner again. Now that they were married, everyone came to the inn for Sunday dinners, and it was always a fun time since guests often joined them. Of course, those were the Sundays they were all on their best behavior, hoping for repeat business.

"Need help with anything?" SuAnn asked as she walked into the kitchen.

"Nope. I think we're good. Is Hen coming today?"

"No, she had to go to some rope cutting ceremony with that boring husband of hers," SuAnn said, taking a piece of the watermelon before Julie could stop her.

"Mom, don't say that."

"She says it herself all the time!"

Everyone had been surprised at what fast friends Henrietta and SuAnn had become. After the whole pie contest debacle, Hen had graciously let everyone know that there was a discrepancy she found in the tally and then stepped down so SuAnn could have the limelight. From then on, the two had spent a lot of time together, always causing a ruckus about something in town. Julie had never seen two women more meant to be best friends than SuAnn and Hen.

"So, William, I hear that you're getting a second boat?" Julie asked as she breezed into the dining room.

"Yep. We're running at least one charter a day, so this could double my business pretty quickly."

"My boyfriend is going to be a gazillionaire and buy me a yacht," Janine joked as she leaned over and kissed his cheek.

"Calm down there, yogi. I think we'll just stick with two fishing boats for awhile."

"Well, I went on one of his charters last weekend, and it was amazing. Caught some huge redfish that day. Dixie grilled them up real nice," Harry said.

"I sure did, and he ate so much he couldn't button his pants!"

Julie walked to the kitchen window and opened it. "Dylan, come in for dinner!"

Dylan, whose adoption was in process, was always running around the property doing this or that. Dawson had taught him a lot about water safety, fishing and even started teaching him to surf. The Department of Children's Services had allowed Dawson and Julie to foster Dylan while the adoption was processing, for which they were very thankful.

Dylan came running through the door, dirty as usual. "I saw a huge crab on the beach!"

"Go wash up, young man," Julie said, rustling his hair. Dylan ran down the hallway to the bathroom.

Julie loved Sundays for this very reason. The house was always full of the people she loved. Vivi, who is now walking, was into everything, so Meg was chasing her all over the living room, trying to keep her out of Dawson's grandmother's priceless antiques.

Colleen and Tucker were sitting on the sofa chatting with Christian about the latest toy that Tucker had invented. It was taking off, and it was poised to be one of the biggest toys of the Christmas season.

"Everybody ready to eat?" Lucy called, popping her head out of the kitchen. If there was one thing that Julie loved, it was having Lucy around. She reminded her of Agnes, her old housekeeper in Atlanta. She had become part of the family, and for that, Julie was grateful.

Everybody sat down around the table as Julie and Lucy brought the food out and set it on the long table. The family was getting bigger and bigger which meant that they had to put the leaves in the table. That was okay with her. She hoped she would need two tables before it was over with.

"Before we get started eating today, I would like to make an announcement," Dawson said. Julie didn't know what he was talking about, so she was eager to hear this secret announcement of his.

"Everybody quiet down," Janine said, patting the chair next to her for Dylan to sit down. She had been a wonderfully calming force for him and had taken on the role as his aunt with gusto, even teaching him some yoga to help him focus at his new school. Thankfully, he'd made plenty of friends there and was no longer being bullied.

"As you all know, we are in the process of making Dylan

an official part of this family," Dawson said. Everybody clapped, and Janine rubbed Dylan's back.

"Julie doesn't even know this, but on Friday, I got a call from the attorney that the adoption is now finalized. You are officially our son!"

Dylan's mouth opened wide and he jumped from his chair, running over to hug Dawson and then Julie.

"Why did you keep this a secret from me?" Julie said, walking over and pinching Dawson on the arm.

"I wanted to see the look on both of your faces."

"So does this mean that I am officially Dylan Lancaster?"

Dawson smiled. "Well, technically, I suppose so. We just have a few papers to file to get your name changed."

"I'm so excited!" Dylan danced around the room, a huge grin on his face.

"Not nearly as excited as we are to have you as our son," Julie said, pulling him over and squeezing him. Being his mother, even for the last few months, had been one of the great joys of her life so far. Tucking him in at night, taking long walks down the beach and reading him stories on the porch were some of her favorite memories so far, and she knew there were thousands more memories to be made.

"Not all families are built by blood, but by love. Here's to family!" Dixie said, holding her glass of sweet tea in the air. Everybody followed and clinked their glasses together.

As the conversations flowed, Julie looked around at all of the people in her life and felt such an immense sense of gratitude. For her husband. Her sister. Her daughters. Her mother. Her friends. And now, for her new son. Life just didn't get any better.

~

Check out more of Rachel Hanna's books including The January Cove Series, The Whiskey Ridge series and The Sweet Tea B&B series!

Made in the USA
Middletown, DE
04 February 2022